Return of the Beastmaster

The World of Valencia

By

S.D. Michaels

The World of Valencia

The World of Valencia

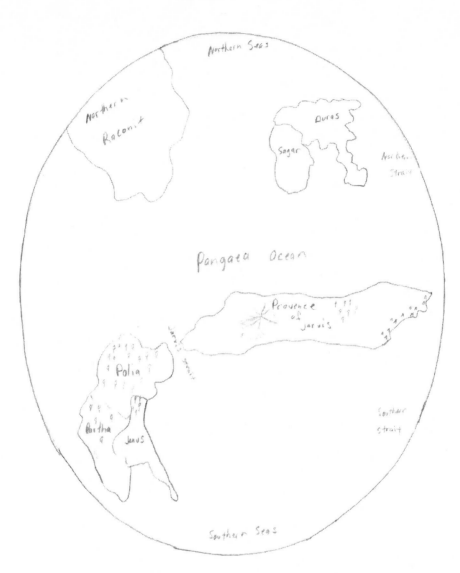

Chapter One

Emily stood in the middle of her office area and looked absentmindedly at the map. Eighteen months, and eight hundred and eighty endangered species later, and her job still wasn't completely done. Now she had to figure out a way to make sure the animals listed as vulnerable or threatened didn't go the way of the Farwest elephant. She should have been figuring out her next plan of attack on how to bring planet-wide conservation to life…but her mind kept wandering back to the Boretra Jaguar that she had seen all those months ago, and started wondering what other animals extinct from Valencia were hidden away on Terra.

Lost in thought, she didn't notice the fog raising around her at first; in fact, it wasn't until it started to impede her sight of the map did she realize she was standing in a cloud bank.

"You are troubled. Come to me," a voice said in the distance.

"I need to get The Young One."

"No, for this journey, you do not."

"How am I supposed to get there? I'm in the middle of my office..."

"Close your eyes, Emily. Clear your mind. I will be here waiting."

Emily closed her eyes and put the Goddess in her mind. Before she realized it, she was standing across from Cathleena in the middle of her white pavilion.

"I know every kind of animal that has left this world because of mankind. Whether or not it be changes that humanity had made to the environment, deliberately or otherwise, it was impossible for them to survive," Cathleena said sorrowfully.

Out the corner of her eye, Emily spotted another figure and acknowledged her with a nod. Slightly shorter, but with the same brilliant blonde hair and body structure as Cathleena, Ava was awe inspiring but you could tell she was young and a little immature, because when she joined the two in center of the pavilion, she greeted her older sister with a giggle and a big hug. "I'm so excited," she proclaimed. "I don't know all the creatures that father put on my world yet. But Cathleena said she would teach me about them if I allow you to join us on Terra for the lessons."

Emily turned with excitement. "I'm going to Terra?"

"You asked about the animals gone from Valencia?"

Emily pulled out her phone. "Can I take pictures?"

The two goddesses exchanged puzzled looks. "I see no reason why you cannot," Cathleena said finally.

Ava stepped up next to her sister and the three disappeared from Valencia and reappeared on Terra. Emily looked around her at first thinking that nothing had happened. They were still standing in the middle of a pavilion, but this one only had one throne and was slightly smaller.

"Come with me," Ava said, dashing down the steps into the clearing that surrounded the marble structure. "Where should we start? Ocean, mountains, how about the woods to the east, or the icepacks? Yes, the icepacks, you don't have those on Valencia anymore, right?" Ava kept talking as she raced away from them.

Emily chuckled at Cathleena's shocked expression. "She's excitable, isn't she?"

"Yes, she is," Cathleena said, elegantly gliding across the white stone floor and down the steps onto the clearing.

The day was beautiful. The sun was out, not a cloud in the sky, there was a slight breeze coming out of the west. Emily took in a deep breath. She felt high on the fresh air, no smog or smoke. No stench of the city, the air was clean and pure. It was so serene. Everywhere she looked was utterly beautiful, she was amazed. There was no noise outside that of nature; it was so peaceful that all she wanted to do was lay down in the tall grass and just take it all in. Ava encouraged her to follow, and everywhere they went, every living creature all the way down to the smallest insect and the gnomes that lived in that area came out to surround the human and the two Goddesses that had come to visit. She got to see some of her old gnome friends like Ptilopsis, Vulpes and Chelonia, and some new ones as well, and better than all of that she also got the privilege to get an up close look at some of Terra's largest and most powerful predators. Tigers, Bears, Lions, and even the Boretra Jaguar came out to greet them and get their picture taken by the biologist.

Emily had knowledge of a lot of the animals, but it was all from books or lectures at school. The goddesses, especially Cathleena, seemed to have a personal relationship with each and every beast. Cathleena carried them across the surface of Terra and into the depths of its oceans, pointing out creatures that neither Ava nor Emily had ever seen before. In the south Emily looked out across the rolling prairie at a herd of what she had thought where were wild white horses feeding in the tall grasses. That was until she spotted the horn protruding from the forehead of the one nearest to them.

Startled, she looked at Cathleena. "No way! Unicorns? I thought they were a myth?"

Cathleena turned to her raising a brow. "You said the same about me once, I believe."

Emily ignored the remark. "Were they ever on Valencia?"

Cathleena nodded, and pointed to the little creatures fluttering around the herd. "Those too were once on our planet."

Emily squinted, then looked back over to the goddess. "Fairies? I suppose you have some Pegasus over in the next pasture?" she said with sarcasm.

Cathleena gave her a puzzling look.

"You know, winged horses. Pegasus," she teased.

"Oh, the flying horses are in the mountains. I'll show you when we get over there," Ava squeaked excitedly.

Emily shook her head, trying to take it all in. "I don't suppose you have any flaming birds around here?"

"There are birds of fire in the land to the west," Ava replied mystified. "I've seen those myself."

Emily met Cathleena's gaze. "So, all those creatures in mythology actually existed at one time or another on Valencia?"

"I'm not sure what creatures you're talking about, but yes, they probably did. Our world has lost more than half of the creatures my father had put on there."

"Ooo, what about the Chupacabra?" Emily teased. "It's like a hairless dog that supposedly sucks blood from its victims?"

Cathleena chuckled, seeing Emily's smile. "I will show you what dog-like creatures we have, but none suck blood."

So they traveled on. In the woodlands to the south, they came across a small grizzly-type bear, that came to mid-thigh and that weighed less than a hundred pounds. It was also no longer found on Valencia, another victim feared and hunted by humans until they existed no more.

In the north they looked over mass areas of ice and snow and saw a large pack of pure white wolf, a few foxes also in their white winter coats, seals, polar bears, caribou, musk ox, and even a snow hare scurrying across the frozen tundra followed closely by a snow owl. All were normally found in the frozen north, but no longer on Valencia because of the melting of the ice caps from global warming.

On the Faiji Islands, Cathleena brought them face to face with the strangest creature of all. It was about the size and shape of a large dog. Emily had to think back through her school year days to try to remember what the beast was called. Some kind of tiger, though it wasn't really a tiger at all. If she remembered right, it had more in common with the kangaroo than the tiger, but it also had stripes, so people went with the visual cues when it came to naming it. It was a marsupial, meaning that it had a pouch in which to carry its young. It had gone extinct on the mainland over a thousand years ago and was only found on the smallest island in the Faiji chain up until 1933. The last one was captured and put in the City of Toft zoo, where it lived until its death in 1936. She remembered seeing a picture of it, and recalled that after its death they had it stuffed it and placed it in the Toft museum where it is still on display to this day.

Since her phone was too big for the gnomes to handle, and feeling that it would be improper to ask either goddess to take a picture of her with an animal, Emily resorted to a lot of selfies with her new furry friends close by her side. She got a picture of herself with an unusual looking Flying Fox, and one an Ivory-Billed Woodpecker, a Giant Galliwasp (which is a type of large lizard), a Faiji Dolphin, and a Faijian Leopard, all lost now from the Faiji Islands on her world.

After visiting the Islands, Cathleena took them through the plains, where huge herds of elephants roamed across the grasslands. Moving to a smaller group by the watering hole, Cathleena walked amongst them, greeting each of her precious children.

"Are those the ones from Valencia?" Emily asked.

Ava nodded, her eyes showing her excitement. "It was hard for her to let them go. She would have preferred to have them stay on her planet."

"Yeah," Emily said looking around her. "I would have liked that, too."

Emily has no idea how long she'd been gone, her picture-taking came to a stop when her battery died in her phone. And that was toward the beginning of the trip. Cathleena took them around the globe and introduced them both to every creature her father ever created that burrowed, walked, crawled, slithered, jumped, swam, or flew. Emily lost track of which animal was new solely because it had never been discovered and which one she didn't know about because of its extinction. It was a lot, though, and this little trip with the goddesses only renewed her need to change things on her planet so that they could keep what animals were left there.

Leaving Ava behind on Terra, Cathleena and Emily returned to Valencia. As they stood once more on the edge of the pavilion looking out over their world, Emily decided that it was a good time for her to get some answers to questions that had been bothering her, so she turned to the goddess Cathleena and said, "What's your father like? I mean, he created all those magnificent things, the ground, the sky, the insects, the animals, the plants. He must be very warm and caring?"

"To the contrary," Cathleena laughed. "He's neither."

"How can that be?"

"Let's see if I can say this is in a way you'll understand." Cathleena collected her thoughts, taking a deep breath as she began. "Jabaz is all powerful, but how he came into being, none of us know. After millenniums of being alone and wandering in an empty void, he decided to use his power to fill his loneliness. First he created our mother Nia, then he created the heaven from which they would reign. And so it was at the beginning, he and she ruled side by side. But there was nothing for them to govern over, so he created the first of his worlds. Some he made of just land, others of just water, there were others of both and a few with neither, they just being balls of gas. After a time, he found the combination that pleased him. And much as he does to this day, he made land and water, and put creatures to swim in the water and ones to fill the skies and crawl upon the earth. After many more millenniums he grew bored of this too, and made mortal man in his image. For unlike his other creations, he gave man the ability to understand and to worship his creator, and this pleased father very much. He made many worlds, more than neither he nor our mother cared to watch over. So with Nia's suggestion they started a family of immortals to help watch over and care for his creations for all time. None of us know for sure how many offspring the God of Creation and the Queen of the Underworld had, some say thousands, and some say many more."

"Why did you call your mother the Queen of the Underworld?"

"My mother fell out of favor with her husband a very long time ago. He made the mistake when he created her of making her strong-willed and she would argue with him often, especially when it came to their children. She was banished to the underworld of Valencia to care for the lost souls of the mortals that they had created. Where she has been ever since."

"So he likes to banish people if they do something he doesn't like?"

Cathleena turned to face Emily. "He is the supreme being. There is no other above him."

Emily lowered her gaze briefly, then glanced up at her again. "What happened to you guys?" she asked, in a pleading tone. "Why did you give up on us?"

Cathleena's face became strained. "Adele was so many things to us, one being peacemaker. She kept us from fighting all the time. My sister and I."

"Zorine?"

"Yes. Zorine had an evil side to her when it came to anything that lived and breathed. After Adele's banishment, those humans she was placed in charge of started to suffer. Adele could see it happening and so could Sabvon. They begged for me to intervene, but I was weak and afraid of Zorine's wrath. In the end it was our mother who requested of our father for us to be released as guardians of this world."

"Really?"

"You could say that Zorine's neglect was making my mother's job more difficult."

"That's sad."

"Indeed."

"Where is she now?"

"Our father put her where she can do no harm." Cathleena looked at Emily's questioning eyes and continued. "On a forsaken world that has no humans, but savage, green-skinned, primitive humanoid creatures. Tougher, more resilient, capable of living in the harshest of conditions. Very hostile, the clans are always at war with each other. Our father created them and put them on that desolate planet just for her."

"Wow, sounds extreme." Emily thought for a moment then asked. "But what about you, where did you go after you left here?"

"Since I had done nothing wrong, I was left to find my own way. For many years I wandered the cosmos. Went from one world to another. Trying to fit in, but never finding a place in which I belong." Cathleena raised a hand just before Emily spoke. "I know you have many more questions, but there is one who is close to you who can help you find some of the answers. Entrust in her, she's the next step in the healing of our world."

Switching from a bright pavilion to the dank and darkness of the Sacred Valley was a shock. It took a moment for Emily's eyes to adjust, but once they did, she spotted her friend Deb standing by Cathleena's temple.

Emily walked through the overgrown vegetation covering the streets until she was within earshot and called out to her friend. "Deb!"

"Oh, hi," Deb said with a wave.

"Is that all you're going to say?" Emily asked, studying her friend. "Aren't you wondering why you're here?"

"No, but I was wondering why you were. I've had this same dream since I was a kid. I'd come here, stand by the temple awhile, then I'd wake up."

"This isn't a dream, Deb. The Goddess Cathleena sent us here. She said you could answer my question, and that you were the next step in the healing of our world."

Deb looked bewildered as she took in her surroundings.

"Deb, did you hear me?" Emily asked, following behind her as she started to wander.

"I should have woken up by now," she said touching the monolith in front of the temple. "This feels so real."

Emily pointed to the glyphs that Deb's hand rested by. "Tell me what those mean," she said, moving up beside her. "You know how to read those, right? Didn't your parents teach you?"

Deb turned around and looked at her friend. "Okay, I get it. That's why I've been coming here all this time. To tell you what this means."

"Yes," Emily said excitedly. "Can you read it for me? What do the glyphs mean?"

"It's a temple dedicated to the goddess Cathleena."

"I know that, but what do the marks mean?"

"This temple was erected by a follower of hers called the Beastmaster. The paw print was his mark."

"Wait a minute, what's Cathleena's symbol?"

"It's this one," she said, pointing to another glyph. "It's the deer standing in front of the oak tree. Or in some cases there's just the oak tree. Or maybe it's the tree of life. I'm not sure, but that's her mark."

Emily looked at the symbol on her chest. "This is that mark. But you and Ptilopsis told me I was touched by a goddesses. Who in the heck's mark is this, if it's not Cathleena's? Is it Adele's, or Zorine's, maybe it's Ava?"

"Okay wait, we were kids. I'm not perfect, and who's Ptilopsis, are you telling me that you've been talking to an owl? And who's Ava?"

"No. I've been talking to a gnome that looks like an owl. And Ava is the goddess of Terra. She the younger sister to Cathleena and all those others." Emily sighed and sat down heavily on one of the broken walls. "You're not helping me at all. Cathleena told me you'd be able to answer my question."

Deb stood for a moment studying her friend then said. "This is really strange. I'm usually awake by now."

"It's not a dream, Deb. For some reason, you and I have been chosen to fix our world. For the past eighteen months, I've been moving the endangered animals off Valencia and onto another planet called Terra, and trying to teach the world about conservation. I had six gnomes living in my house up until last month and one that's still there, which I can't keep out of trouble. He's like having a three year old running around." Emily sighed. "I've talked to the Goddesses Cathleena and Ava. Ava is kind of young but they're both pretty cool to be around. Neither has asked me to worship them, because that would be awkward. I've traveled to Terra and got to see every animal that their father Jabaz created."

Emily moved over to the shrine and looked at the glyphs once more. "I was talking to her about what had happened to them after Adele's banishment. She told me about herself, she told me about Zorine…And then she sent me here."

Emily glanced back over at her friend who had a look of total astonishment on her face. Walking over to her, she grabbed Deb's shoulders and shook her. "You've got to work with me here, Deb. Cathleena said you could help me."

Deb started to stutter, and Emily shook her again. "Come on, Deb. You were the one who said you believed in all this stuff. Now think. Why would Cathleena send us here?"

"Adele."

"What about Adele?"

"Did she tell you why Adele was banished?"

"No, she didn't tell me anything about her."

"She fell in love with a human. Which was a big no-no if you were one of Jabaz's children." Deb led Emily through the streets of the ancient civilization. "Adele's punishment was for her and her child to be made mortal. My parents tracked her from Rasdor to this village." The two women stepped into what used to be a twenty by forty foot room on the outskirts of the town. At the front of the room laid two large slabs of stone. She pointed to the stone on the left. "Adele's mark was that of a swaddling child in its mother's arms. Like this one here," she said pointing to the glyph. "Zorine's mark was a thunder cloud with a lightning bolt through it. None of those were ever found in this village. I don't know who Ava is or what her mark is, but the mark that's on you is that of the Beastmaster. It's written that he was a Demi god banished to a life of mortality along with his mother. The Goddess Adele." Deb pointed to the slab on the right.

Emily knelt beside the stone and looked at the elemental symbols that decorated the top and sides. In the center was a large paw print. A strange feeling came over her, forcing her to back away from the stone. "What is this place?"

Deb was holding herself, as if to fight off the cold. "A

crypt, I think."

Chapter Two

Emily handed Deb a cup of coffee and leaned back against her desk.

"So this is the war room, huh?" Deb said, spinning the chair around to look at the map on the wall.

"We're not at war." Tegula said, climbing up to the desk top.

Emily chuckled, remembering the days of collaboration between her and her Gnome friends. "Yeah, this is where we decided which animals we were going to move them to Terra, and when. These were the first ones moved."

"Wait. There's no more Farwest elephants on Valencia?"

"Just the ones in the zoos and reserves, and a couple of babies in Rainobi that I got to meet, but they were orphaned and wouldn't have made it in the wild."

Deb gave Emily a frown. "That stinks."

"Yeah I know," Emily sighed. "But I got to see them on Terra. They're alive and well, and safe from poachers."

Tegula moved up next to Emily and tugged on her sleeve, "You're supposed to be giving a speech soon at the Cultural Heritage Center, on protection and restoration of the world's ecosystem."

"He's cute," Deb said, gently poking Tegula's tummy. "Nature gnomes, makes perfect sense."

"What does?" Emily asked.

"That the goddesses chose gnomes to help you." Deb saw the look of confusion on Emily's face and continued. "You really need to sit in on some of my dad's lectures. Okay, listen. Jabaz created our world by using magic. Therefore, our world is magic, everything in it is magic. It's in us, all around us. Our ancestors had the ability to tap into it. For some reason, today we can't." She looked thoughtfully for a moment, and then continued. "Nature gnomes are one with nature. Like our ancestors, they have the ability to tap into the magic."

Emily straightened the shell on Tegula's head. "Well, I've got to go," she said finally. "Seems all I'm doing these days is giving speeches on saving the planet." Looking over at Deb, she added, "You going to be okay while we're gone? I suppose we could take you home first."

"Go," Deb said, getting back on the computer. "I'm going to see what else I can find out about this guy they called the Beastmaster."

Upon their return, Emily and Tegula were greeted by a somber friend who was still staring at the computer screen, going over file after file of forgotten and lost cities. "Do you know how many civilization we've lost from our world?"

Emily glanced at Tegula, and then back to Deb. "No."

"Thirty-four lost cities so far, forgotten by time and man," she said, spinning around in her chair. "But lucky for us, it looks like the ones in the Northeast, from the Old forest of Dane to the High Reaches are the only ones that mention a saver, or a Master of the Beast, as some referred to him. And that covers about five different sites. Sacred Valley, you and I have already been there. Punasia, also in the Forest of Shadows, Ciupap south of Mount Maygar, Xanila at the upper tip of Tehys, and Cybele in the Old forest of Dane."

"Old forest of Dane, that place is cursed."

"I know my parents hated going there," Deb shrugged. "We'll save that for last."

"You up for an adventure, little buddy?" Emily asked Tegula. "We should go check out those sites."

Tegula nodded, moved on top of the desk and watched Emily.

Emily printed up a picture of each site and started by studying the picture of the ruins of Punasia. Once she had it in her mind, she took Deb's hand and felt Tegula's hand touching her on the side. "Ready?"

It's hard to imagine how an entire civilization can disappear, but that's exactly what has happened to Punasia. Lost and forgotten in time until it was rediscovered by an archaeologist a couple hundred years ago. Like Sacred Valley, much of forgotten city had been reclaimed by the forest after the archaeologist had left. According to Deb, there were no artifacts found at this site, seemingly to mean that it was a planned move and the villagers took everything with them when they left. But why, no one knew. Tegula pointed to a small pillar which to an outsider looked like a tree trunk sticking out of the ground. After getting a better look at it, Deb pointed out the glyphs and the symbol of the Beastmaster.

"It's magical," Tegula said, placing his hand on it. "This was placed here by a person of great power."

Emily knelt beside him and examined the carvings. "Can you read these glyphs, Deb?"

Deb was already beside her, brushing dirt and moss from the stone. "It's a marker. All it says is that this is a meeting place.

"A meeting place for what?"

"For him," Deb said. "The Beastmaster. This is one of the places people came to see, and hear him speak."

"I wonder what he talked about."

"Maybe the same things that you do at your little speeches."

After exchanging a look, the two women searched around for a while before Emily stopped and pulled another picture out of her pocket. "There's nothing here. Let's try this one."

Ciupap consists of a series of terraces carved into the mountainside, a net of stoned roads and several small circular plazas. "Ancestors of the original occupants believe it was the heart of a network of villages inhabited by their forebears," Deb said, reading the notes she had written down about each site. "After the climate changed, becoming much colder and wetter, the settlement was abandoned by its residents who moved to lower elevations."

"There's nothing here, either. No wall, no pillar, nothing above ground to hold the mark of the Beastmaster," Emily said, with a look of frustration.

"Look from up here," Tegula called down from the hillside. "It looks like a paw print from up here."

Emily climbed higher up on the mountain and looked down over the site. Sure enough, the circular plazas were laid out in the shape of a paw print. "I guess I've got to stop yelling at you for wandering off. I never would have seen it from down there."

"Were there any artifacts for here, Deb?"

"No. Besides the flat stones used for the plazas and the roads, the scientist found nothing here. All materials came from the mountain itself. Nothing was brought in from anywhere else."

"Another meeting place?"

Deb shrugged. "Maybe."

"Well, let's try a different site." Pulling out another picture, Emily studied it for a moment.

Xanila, an ancient city nestled between the Upper and Lower Maygar River. "The city degenerated into anarchy shortly after the banishment of Adele," Deb said, reading what she could of the ancient writing. The walls were covered with glyphs. "It says it flourished once again when the saver, Master of the Beast, brought peace and salvation back to the region. He's credited with repairing or rebuilding the temples of their world's two remaining goddesses," Deb sighed, and tried rubbing the dirt out of the cracks. "The rest is really hard to read."

Emily looked around her. All that remained of the city today was a mound of broken mud-brick buildings and piles of debris in the fertile land between the two rivers.

"So he tried helping his people by reconnecting them to their goddesses," Emily said softly.

"Yeah, these people were at war with neighboring villages," Deb said. "He basically stopped the fighting and got them to focus on helping each other. He taught them how to grow corn, squash, beans, potatoes, avocado, tomatoes, and chili peppers."

"But what happened to them?"

"Look at the building, Em. This damage is more modern, this is rubble from a city that had been bombed. I'll have to look it up when we get home, but I'll bet because of its location and all, I'd say it got hit in the Great War."

Emily pulled out the last picture, Cybele, in the Old forest of Dane.

Everything in the Old forest of Dane was big. Huge, rugged, grey tree trunks grew all around them, some as wide around as a small house, others sporting mansion-sized girths. The sun, for all its effort, barely made it through the thick green canopy above. Its meandering light touched the ground just enough to show them the moss and dead leaves that littered the forest floor covering what appeared to be a stone road that led up to an primeval ghost town, with its view partially hidden by the jungle in which it was made.

"Do you hear that?" Emily asked, straining her ears.

"I don't hear a thing."

"That's just it. There's no animal noises, no birds, frogs, squirrels, monkeys, no wind blowing through the trees. There's nothing." Emily was spooked enough as it was, and when Deb grabbed for her hand for comfort, she screamed. "Dang it, Deb. Don't do that."

"Sorry, but this places gives me the hebe-jebe's."

"You and me both," Emily said, shaking off her touch. "This whole place is creepy."

"Wait, what are you doing?" Deb asked, as Emily started walking towards the first opening in the trees. "I don't think we should go in there."

"We've got to go in. Look, the archaeologist went in right?"

"Yeah, and there were over a dozen of them and it was hundreds of years ago. It's just you and me here right now, and I'm scared to death."

Emily patted her friend's shoulder. "We're not alone. We've got Tegula. Tell her buddy, tell her this place isn't as bad as it looks."

The little gnome put his back against Emily's leg. "There was great evil here once…" he said, staring blankly ahead.

"That's not what I wanted you to tell her."

"It has been contained and its control of the forest neutralized by someone with great power, but you can still feel its presence. It still hungers."

"Hungers for what? Deb asked in a shaky voice.

"Flesh."

Deb screamed and ran back to the end of the path. Emily looked from her to Tegula. "That wasn't very smart, now we'll never get her inside."

Tegula gave her apologetic shrug and attached himself to Emily's leg. "Not you too?" she said, with disgust.

"I don't like this place," he said nervously.

Emily had to drag her leg that Tegula was hanging onto to get over to Deb. "What did the archaeologist's report say about this place?" she asked her.

Deb pulled out the paper with shaky hands.

"Was there artifacts?" Emily asked.

"Yes. It says the building were all intact and contents as well. It also says that nothing was removed from the site, because they weren't able to."

"What is that supposed to mean?"

"I don't know. It doesn't say."

"How do you know the Beastmaster was even here?"

"Because the report says his mark is all over the place."

Emily looked back over to the city. "Come on," she said, picking up Tegula and grabbing Deb's hand. "We're going in."

"Wait!" Ptilopsis said, racing in front of them. Within seconds five little gnomes converged onto the road ahead of them.

Emily was startled at the sudden appearance of her little friends. "Where did you guys come from?"

"Terra," Ptilopsis replied.

"That's not what I meant. Why are you here?"

Tegula bit his bottom lip and looked away from Emily's gaze. "I might have called them."

"What?"

"Sorry. I was scared." Tegula wiggled his way out of her arms and gathered with his gnome friends on the path.

Deb stepped up next to Emily. "Wow. You said there was six and there they are."

The two women watched in amazement. Like a football team strategizing their next play, they huddled in the middle of the road and then ran off and disappeared into the surrounding forest.

"Where did they go?" Emily asked.

Deb shook her head. "I don't see them, anywhere," she said frantically. "This isn't good. How are we going to get back? You can call Cathleena, can't you?"

Emily cocked her head and looked at her friend. "Don't panic, let's give them a minute, okay?"

Both women screamed and tucked when they heard the cracking of hundreds of branches overhead. Like a light being switched on in a room, the sun shone through the now opening canopy and illuminated the ground below. Emily and Deb held each other as the earth trembled from the mighty trees twisting, pulling, and bending their colossal branches and trunks, back and out of the way of the midday sun.

Emily spotted Ptilopsis and the others coming out of the forest and ran to them. "What just happened here?"

"The evil is kept at bay by the light. So we asked the trees to move so the sun could shine through."

"You're a genius," she said, scooping him up and kissing his cheek. "Now we can go in, and actually see where we're going."

"Plus the light makes it not so dark and gloomy," Deb said sheepishly.

Emily put Ptilopsis down. Looking around her, she said, "Where did the others go?"

"Back to Terra. You'll be safe now."

"Wait! Don't go," Emily said kneeling down next to Ptilopsis. "I could really use your help."

"I know. Ava has said that I can stay as long as there is need."

"Cool," Emily sighed. Looking over at her grinning friend she said. "Ptilopsis, this is Deb, my friend. Deb, this is the Wise One whom I call Ptilopsis."

"I can see the resemblance to the owl," she whispered. "Hello," she said aloud.

Ptilopsis bowed, and extended his arm in the direction to the city. "The path is clear. Shall we go?"

Emily led the way down the widening street. Stopping at the edge of the tree line, she craned her head back to look up into the canopy. Now that there was light coming in, she could see the tops of the trees, and they had to be over two to three hundred feet tall. But the most impressive thing was not the magnificent city in front of them, but the giant statue of a man in simple clothing with a jaguar cub draped across his shoulders, a snake wrapped around his waist, and a bird of prey perched on his forearm.

"This must be the Beastmaster," Emily said, in awe.

"Wow, I wish my folks were here, they'd die to see this."

Emily touched Deb's shoulder to acknowledge her excitement, and walked past the statue and up to the gates of the walled city. Putting a hand to the wooden planks on the right she pushed in slightly and watched the gate swing inward silently.

"Okay," Deb said from behind her. "We're back to this being creepy."

Emily sucked in a breath to still her pounding heart. Stepping through the opening, she looked out into courtyard. To the right was a temple to Cathleena much like the ones they had seen at the other abandoned villages, but this one was in pristine condition.

"It's all protected by magic," Ptilopsis said. "Very powerful magic.

"Evil?" Deb asked.

"No. I sense no danger here."

Emily moved farther inside. "This site is supposed to be over two thousand-years old, but it looks like it was just built yesterday. How can this be?"

"Awesome!" Deb said, as she joined Emily inside the gate. "And we never knew about it because it was hidden away in the haunted forest."

"That was the whole idea," said a voice from the side.

Emily spun around to face the owner of the voice. In front of her stood a dark haired man with piercing green eyes in his early twenties, with tennis shoes, baggy pants and punk-rocker T-shirt.

Emily looked down and gave Ptilopsis a questioning look. "Why didn't you warn us, and why are you still here?"

"I didn't see any need of a warning, and I can show myself to him because he's magic."

"Magic? Did you do all this?"

"Not me. Our forefathers created this sanctuary."

"Sanctuary for what?"

The young man shrugged and gave her a smile. Turning he said, "For anyone in need."

From all over the courtyard, people and animals appeared, seemingly out of nowhere. "Welcome to Cybele," the young man said, holding his arms open wide.

"Look," an old woman yelled from the back. "The divine one has sent an omen."

Emily looked to where the woman was pointing. Ptilopsis smiled. "Maybe we should find out who the divine one is?" he whispered.

"Cathleena, of course," the young man answered the gnome's inaudible question. "They call me Tristan. And you are a child of nature, but not of this world, I think. We are most honored, just the same. Come, let me show you around."

"You have an unusual name," Emily replied.

"It's what they gave me when I came here. My birth name is Dolphus."

Deb mumbled the man's name and stopped Emily as she started following him. "Sipen, for noble-wolf."

"Ah, you know the old tongue?" The young man said as he turned back to look at her.

Deb shifted uneasily. "Just what we learned in school."

"That's cool. I went to some of the finest schools there are, but never had the chance to learn the languages of our ancestors."

"You didn't take the right classes," Emily said. "It's used all the time in science."

"Well see, that's the problem," he grinned. "I'm lousy at science. I was more into the arts. Like the art of not studying. Come on, we can talk while we walk."

"So way did they change your name?" Deb asked.

"In an attempt to leave my old life behind," he laughed. "But truthfully, I didn't much care for my birth name."

"But your family is special in society."

"My family disowned me when I was twelve. Come, there is much for you to see."

Everywhere she looked, Emily saw people from all walks of life and all nationalities living and working side by side. Cybele was far from modern, but every need for every person and animal was met. There were smiths, bakers, millers, farmers, weavers, craftsmen, beekeepers, herders, horse groomers, fish mongers, tailors, cobblers, glaziers, stone cutters, herbalist, alchemist, healers, and teachers. "Where did all these people come from, and how did they learn how to do all this stuff?"

Tristan pointed across the street to a shop that made pottery. An older woman was teaching two children the art of painting vases. "Those who first came to Cybele brought the knowledge with them, now all traits are passed down from a master to their apprentices." Stopping at an eatery, he gestured for Emily and Deb to sit down. After flat bread, cheese, fruit and cups of water were brought out to them, he continued. "People come here from all over. I myself came here from Topios a couple of years ago after blowing up a car."

"So what happened? Your family kicked you out and you became some kind of delinquent?" Emily spat.

"Yeah, you could say that. I belonged to a gang and was living on the streets for many years until the day that the incident happened. The car I destroyed was being driven by a boy from a rival street gang. He had already gone past us and shot down two of my friends. He was coming back to finish off the rest of us."

"And you blew up the car?" Deb asked.

"With a single thought." he replied solemnly.

"You didn't throw anything at it, like a gas bomb or grenade?" Emily asked.

Emily met Tristan's gaze. He could see the doubt in her eyes and laid his hand flat on the table, palm up. "Ignite," he said softly. Both girls jumped back when a tongue of flame leap up and started dancing on his open hand without burning him. "Ice," he said, sending a layer of frost over his hand extinguishing the fire.

"Holy cow," Deb gasped.

"I couldn't keep my buddies quiet, they knew it was me. They'd seen me do the fire thing before. So once word got out about me blowing up the car, I got pretty popular. With the cops, and every other government agency out there."

"Cool," Deb said. "You're a sorcerer."

"A sorcerer?" Emily said, doubtfully. "You mean like a magician?"

Tristan shook his head, "Not an illusionist, like you see in the show circuits that travel around. I'm a user of magic."

"But not all these people are users of magic?" Emily asked, as she looked around.

"No, some were born here, some have been here since the great quake, others lost their homes when the economy crashed a few years ago. Then there's the ones who were bullied in school. And of course there's ones like me who have the authorities after them. We have wild animals here who have lost their habitats to logging, a few who were injured by cars, some who were once pets and were neglected, beaten, starved or abused in others ways by their former owners. Then there's people that are gifted and drawn here. Like you, I'm assuming."

"I'm not gifted," Emily said with a start.

"You travel with gnomes," he pointed out.

"And she has the mark of the Beastmaster," Deb added, nonchalantly.

"Deb!" Emily scolded.

"Really?" he asked.

Deb shrugged. "What?"

"I can't believe you told him that?"

"You have the mark of the city's savior. You really are special."

"And she's friends with the goddess Cathleena."

"Deb!"

"What?"

Tristan fell to his knees. "I'm sorry, I did not know," he said, touching her shoe. "I beg your forgiveness, Holy One."

Emily pulled her foot away from Tristan. Her eyes stared to dart around at their surroundings. People were starting to migrate over to where they were sitting. "Get up, and stop that. I am not the holy one," she said in a soft but firm voice. "You're drawing a crowd. Much as what your buddies did with you and the cops."

"But you are friends with the Goddess, you're a priestess then?"

Emily straightened, pulling Tristan up with her. "I know her, it's true, but we are not friends. I'm not a priestess. I'm not the holy one."

"But you bear the mar--"

"Stop, please. People are staring."

Emily glared at Deb who was covering her mouth with her hands.

"Sorry," she whispered.

"Can you take us to the gate, Tristan?"

"You can't leave," he whimpered. "I'm sorry if I angered you."

Emily looked around at the group of people gathering. In the middle was an older man who contended to push to the front.

Emily called Tegula's name and grabbed Deb's hand. Shaking her head sadly at Tristan, she thought of home.

Chapter Three

"No. I did not want him coming with us. Take him back," Emily shouted at the gnomes.

"But you didn't get your answers," Ptilopsis said, climbing up onto the desk top next to Tegula. "Besides he didn't bring him, I did."

"He thinks I'm a priestess or something." Emily glanced over and saw Deb talking to Tristan. "Get away from him," she yelled at her friend. "And stop telling him my life story. You've caused enough trouble."

"Hey," Deb said, with a surrendering gesture. "He was confused, I was just trying to set him straight."

"Of course he's confused. You're telling him all those crazy things about me, how's he supposed to understand any of it?"

"Listen, babe, I'm not from the dark ages you know. I understand plenty."

Emily listen to his outburst then started to laugh. "It's a good thing I'm not what you thought I was, or I might take offence to you calling me babe."

Tristan cowered behind Deb. "Sorry," he mumbled.

Emily paced for a moment as she went over her options. "Okay," she said at last. "Tell me what you know about the Beastmaster."

"You mean the statue in the front court yard of Cybele?"

"Yes, that guy."

"He and his family founded the city for people in need. He's known by many names; the savior, the master of the beast, the beastmaster. He was a servant of the goddesses of nature."

"I know all that," Emily said in frustration. "Tell me something I don't know."

"How much do you know about the Old forest of Dane?"

Emily glared at him.

"Okay," he said, shifting his stance. "Ah, the forest is inhabited by evil shadows. The Beastmaster and his family magically neutralized the evil by trapping the shadows into the trees and used the commoners' fear of the forest to create a haven for themselves, and then as time went on it became a safe place for anyone in need. At the time it was them that were in need. Cybele was named so followers of the goddesses could find her here. It means city of Adele, in the old language."

"Why would they need a safe haven?"

"Because people found out who she really was and blamed her for the damnation that had fallen upon the world."

Emily had a look of surprise on her face. "They turned on her?"

"Some, but a few still saw her as a goddess and were loyal to her to the end."

"To the end. What happened to her?" Emily asked.

"If you want the whole story, you have to go back to Cybele."

"Why can't you tell us?" Deb asked.

"Because I don't know what happened to her."

Emily started to pace. "You saw those people, the way they looked at me. It's not safe for me back there."

"That was my fault and I'm sorry. It's just that they've been waiting for the return of the savior for a long time."

"Oh great, so now you're going to pass me off as the savior."

Tristan held his arms out in a helpless gesture. "I don't know what to call you, but I know that you're special. Please come back Cybele with me and talk to the Keeper of the Records. He's the only one that can help you on this quest of yours."

"Records? What kind of records?"

"Records of their lives."

"Whose lives?"

"The goddess Adele and her family. There's dozens of records about their encounters and struggles during their travels. I'm sorry I didn't listen to the elders as much as I should have, history is not my strong point."

"Nor science from what you said," Deb huffed.

Emily looked over at Deb and thought for a moment, eventually she moved up to Tristan and grabbed his hand. "We're going to do a little experiment," she said signaling the others to join her. After feeling the gnomes by her side she said. "Close your eyes and picture the place that holds all the records. Do you see it in your mind?"

"Yes."

Once they entered the room Emily looked around at her surrounding, its walls were full of shelving loaded down with every kind of book, tome and scroll imaginable, and in the middle of the room sat a scholarly gentleman with glasses reading over pieces of parchment spread out on the table in front of him. "You can open your eyes now," she said softly to Tristan. "I think we're here."

"Teleportation," Tristan said in awe. "If only I could travel like that all the time. I'd be a great wizard."

Emily tapped on his shoulder and pointed at the elderly man who was now staring at them over the top of his glasses.

Tristan glanced over and smiled. "Oh. Yeah. That's the Keeper of the Records, Lemuel."

"Well, this is kind of awkward," Deb whispered to Emily, as they waved at the older man.

Lemuel removed his glasses and studied the trio. "You, I've seen before," he said pointing his spectacles at

Tristan. "But you two must be new here, I don't remember seeing you before."

"You're right. They are new," Tristan said, moving away from the two ladies. "This is Emily and Deb. They're interested in the Beastmaster. I told them about the records."

The scholar pulled a walking stick out from under his desk and slowly moved to the far side of the room. "It goes left to right, oldest to newest. They're all a couple thousand years old, so I hope your ancient tongue is sharp. They're all written in the old language."

Emily pulled down a tube and opened it up, handing the scroll that was inside to Deb. She heaved a sigh. "You're better at this than me."

Deb unrolled the scroll and looked over the text. "Can you read this?" she asked the scholar.

"I'm assuming you cannot?" Lemuel asked, raising a brow.

Both Emily and Deb shook their heads. "My dad might be able to," Deb said.

"He's not here, is he?" the scholar asked.

"No," Deb sighed.

"Then you have a problem. People can come and go from Cybele, but artifacts cannot."

"Why can't they?"

"To protect the magic."

Emily and Deb exchanged looks again, then Deb turned back to the Record Keeper. "Can you read this?"

"Yes."

Deb checked her temper and smiled. "Can you tell us what they say or, are you willing to teach us how to read them?"

"I have not read them, so no, I cannot tell you. And it takes years to be able to read the ancient tongues. There are six in all, just figuring out which one you're looking at is half the battle."

Emily's shoulders slumped as she sat down heavily in the chair.

"You don't have any quicker courses, do you?" Deb asked.

"Seek out Manalia," he said gathering the scrolls. "She will have what you need to read them."

"A potion! Of course," Tristan said, with a snap of his finger. "Manalia is the village alchemist. She can make you a potion so you can read that stuff."

Lemuel nodded and handed the scrolls to Deb and Emily. "He can show you the way," he said pointing at Tristan. "Though it might be best to use the front door with Manalia."

Emily refocused her eyes and looked again at the parchment. Deb sat next to Tristan rubbing her temples, and groaning loudly. "I've got such a headache."

Tristan stepped up next to woman in a flowery mumu. "This isn't working, Manalia. Are you sure you gave them the right potion?"

"It's the right one, but only one of them is the right person," the old woman said, and moved over to Emily. "Enough. Open your mind. Let the magic work within you."

Emily gave a frustrated sighed, and looked again at the scroll laid out in front of her.

"What do you see?" Manalia asked.

"Symbols, glyphs. Nothing I understand, though."

"Clear your mind. Now start at the beginning. What is this symbol?"

"A.f.t...Wait. Wait. I think I got it. He's writing this."

"He, who?" Manalia asked.

"The son of the goddess Adele. This says after his mother's banishment, human care was split between his two aunts. It says that his mother tried to encourage the people that lived around them to build altars and openly worship the goddesses so that they would know that they were needed, and accept their new roles. She knew her sisters well," Emily said, looking up from the paper. "Cathleena told me that neither of them wanted the humans."

"Do you know what you're doing?" Deb said, shaking her friend. "You're reading it! The potion's working on you."

Emily looked startled, and then puffed herself up. "I can read it. This is cool. Thank you, Manalia."

"Don't thank me yet, and read quickly before the potion wears off."

"How long is that?"

"Hours, days, maybe minutes. Each person is different. Come, let us leave her alone," she said, ushering the others out. "There are wax tablets and stylus next to you for notes."

Emily studied the equipment given to her with which to write. "Ah, Tegula, would you mind going home and getting me a pen and some paper, please?"

After twelve hours Emily called out for something to drink and allowed everyone to come back in. She paced as she went over her notes, taking a sip of water, and translated her scribbles. "Okay, so basically the scrolls were written by Sabvon, son of the goddess Adele, and the wizard Octavian of Rasdor. The first three scrolls are recounts of what happened to Sabvon and his family after his mother's banishment, while they still lived in Rasdor. Like how his father got a job as a tutor to the town's magistrate's two sons. He mentions the birth of his baby sister Aurelia. And how they erected temples to communicate to his two aunts."

Emily took another drink. "Okay, so here's the kicker. Sabvon started hating the humans, he found them useless and insignificant beings and would get into fights constantly with the boys of his town where he lived. Years went by, and then one day his aunt Zorine decided she was done with the humans under her care. It was disaster; crops failed, whole herds died, and people were starving and started to die from some strange sicknesses that was going around. Sabvon's father caught the sickness too, but survived because Sabvon, it seems, still possessed some of his godly powers, like healing. Okay, months go by and one day Sabvon is again fighting with a couple of boys in the town, and they start badmouthing the goddess Adele," Emily said, taking another drink. "You see, ordinary people didn't know that Adele had been banished. They thought she was still in charge of them, and were blaming her for all the bad things that were happening. According to Sabvon, while fighting a group of boys, he nearly kills one with blast of energy to the chest, and in a fit of rage, shouts to the gathering crowd the truth about his mother. Of course the people didn't care that it was really Zorine's fault for the sickness, and they turned on the now powerless Adele, forcing her and her family to flee during the night."

Deb met Emily's gaze. "Wow."

Emily nodded. "Yeah, wow."

"This doesn't sound like the savior of our city," Tristan said.

"The founder of your city was in his early twenties. This one was young, not even a teenager yet. A demi god, whose whole life had been changed in a matter of years. He had one aunt who'd forsaken him and another who couldn't help him. His mother and father were weak, and the people of the village he lived in turned against them."

"His parents were weak?"

"According to Sabvon, his father was but a meager illusionist at best, and Adele lost her godly power and wasn't as good as Sabvon was in tapping into the natural magic of Valencia."

"Why didn't they get sick?" Deb asked.

"Because Adele and her children weren't immortal, but they weren't mortals either. They didn't need much food nor sleep to survive."

"How many of the scrolls did you get through?"

"Almost all of them, but I started getting blurry eyed so I stopped." Emily looked around at her surroundings. "Ah, Tristan, I need to pee. Where are the bathrooms?"

Tristan laughed. "Come on, you're going to love this. Magical toilets, nothing like them in the world."

Chapter Four

Emily was being engulfed by dark tentacles that thrust out of the roots of the trees, shadows that swarmed up her legs and wrapped around her torso and pulled her down. She thrashed out violently, but strong as she was, they overwhelmed her and dragged her onto her back. She landed with a crash and the dirt began to crumble around her.

She has no power here. Take her down and feed…feed…feed!

With a long low tremor, the ground began to rip apart, pulling Emily down with it.

"NO!" Emily screamed, clawing at the earth, trying to pull herself away.

Over the rumble of the trembling ground, a clear ringing voice cut through the trees. "She may not have the power to defeat you," it said. "But I do."

Tall slender shafts of light pierced the forest, lanced the ground, shot up along the trunks of the trees, illuminating them with a blinding blaze of white light like candles soaked in oil. The shadows retreated, howling and gabbling in distress, and the ground heaved and vomited up Emily in an explosion of dirt.

"Come to me," she heard the voice say.

Scrambling to her feet, Emily ran and followed the light through the darkened forest until it came upon a grassy glade and disappeared. Crying and shaken, she staggered and crashed to her knees.

"You're safe now," Cathleena said, appearing in a shimmering glow before her.

"What just happened?" Emily sobbed. "What are those things?"

"They are the shadows of the Old forest of Dane. Lost souls that escaped from the underworld many, many years ago."

"I don't understand."

"You've been reading Sabvon's writings. He and his father had an encounter with the shadows when he was young. Somehow, I believe they used that to get to you."

"But I was asleep in my bed, in Toft!"

"And you still are."

"It was a dream?" she asked, in disbelief. "But it seemed so real."

"The danger was very real, if they had managed to get you underground," Cathleena stopped and with a shudder in her voice. "Nevertheless, you are safe now."

Emily stood and brushed herself off. As she did so, she started hearing voices in her head. "Tegula?"

Cathleena softly chuckled. "Go, he's worried about you."

Emily looked at her hands and saw that they were starting to fade. "Wait," she yelled to the goddess. "You saved my life. Thank you."

Cathleena smiled, and the whole glade burst into a ball of light as she faded away. "You are very welcome," her voice echoed all around. "Now go find your destiny."

Emily sat up in bed, "My destiny. Is that what all of this is about?"

Tegula launched himself into Emily's arms. "You wouldn't wake up! You cried out, and I tried, but I couldn't wake you up."

"I'm okay, little buddy," she said, returning the hug. "I just had a bad dream."

Emily looked over a map of the eastern continent and drew out the path Sabvon and his family took to get to Cybele. After taking a sip of her coffee, she started back into the story of the scrolls that she had been telling to Deb and Tristan. "They followed the same path that Sabvon and his father had taken several years earlier to get to Topios. It ends up that Sabvon had a cousin who was a powerful wizard that lived on Mount Maygar which was under Cathleena's care. And that's where he and his family were heading."

Tristan shook his head, "Didn't know they were related."

"Who?" Deb asked.

"Yorick and the Beastmaster," Emily answered.

"Yorick started the school of magic here. In fact, the Magistrate of Cybele, Josiah, is supposedly a direct descendent of one of Yorick's first students," Tristan said. "Were they related on the goddesses' side?"

Emily nodded. "Like Sabvon, Yorick was a demi god, and his father was Adele's older brother. According to the scrolls, he was imprisoned in his tower by their grandfather, Jabaz. It doesn't say why, though, just that Sabvon helped him escape."

"Wow."

Tristan looked over at Deb. "You say that a lot don't you?"

"What else is there to say, but, wow!"

"Will you two stop?" Emily sighed.

"I didn't start it, he did."

Emily stopped Tristan before he could reply and asked him. "What happened to Yorick?"

"I told you, he started the school here."

"I mean after," she said, standing and moving around the room. "He's a demi god. He could still be alive."

The three looked at each other, then shrugged.

"Wow!" Tristan said.

Deb gave him a questioning look.

"What else is there to say?" he added jokingly.

The three laughed a bit and then Emily moved back over to the map. "The original plan was for all of them to make it to Yorick's fortress," she said in a more serious tone. "Which they did, but after releasing Yorick from his tower they decided to go their separate ways. Yorick, Sabvon, and Aurelia returned to Cybele so that Yorick could train them in magic, but Sabvon's parents traveled on to the Sacred Valley where they lived for many years. He didn't know it at the time, but that would be the last time he'd see either of his folks alive again. His father died ten years later, and once he was gone, Adele lost her will to live, missing her beloved Octavian. With both her sisters gone, her world was falling apart.

So, Adele makes a deal with her mother Nia, goddess of the underworld. Yorick and Sabvon return to

Sacred Valley and make a magical tomb to hold her body. And Adele rejoins her husband for all eternity."

"Creepy," Deb said.

"What, no wow?" Emily asked.

"That's kind of like suicide, isn't it?" Tristan said.

Emily turned on him. "It's romantic."

"Romantic?" he said with a start. "It's pitiful."

Emily moved around the room sweeping her arms as if in a dance. "The whole story of Adele and Octavian is romantic. Beautiful goddess, gives up everything to be with the man she loves."

"Yep, that's a depressing story, alright," Tristan grumbled.

"Forget about him Em," Deb said moving up beside her. "Men have no idea what romance is all about."

Tristan made a bouquet of roses appear in his hand. "I know what romance is," he said, holding out the flowers.

"Then where's the box of chocolates?" Emily asked.

"Oh yeah, you've got to have chocolates," Deb teased, taking the roses from him.

Instantly a box of candy appeared in his empty hand, which Emily promptly took. "Thanks Tristan, that was very nice of you."

"Yeah, Tristan," Deb laughed. "I might have been wrong about you. Maybe you do know a little something about romance."

Emily chuckled as she broke open the box of candy and popped one in her mouth. Setting it down on the table to share with Deb, she turned to the map and started back into her story. "According to the scrolls Sabvon's little sister returned to Cybele where she stayed, but Sabvon left after a couple of years and became nomadic."

Emily glanced back at Tristan, who looked devastated. "Come on, Tristan, we were just joking with you."

Tristan's face had a look of defeat. "You play with my heart, savior, thou hast wounded me." And with that, he disappeared.

Emily and Deb looked at each other both with extreme concern on their faces.

"What just happened here?"

"I think he has a crush on you," Deb said, half-jokingly.

"Not good," Emily gasped. "I didn't know. I was just having fun with him, dang it."

"I know that, but he didn't. You really hurt his feelings. You broke his heart."

You could hear the concern in Emily's voice. "Where did he go?"

Deb shrugged.

"Tristan, I'm sorry," Emily yelled. "Please come back."

Within seconds, Tristan reappeared with laughter booming all around the room. "Got you."

Emily looked at him with a perplexed gaze.

"I was just having fun with you," he laughed.

"I thought you left." she said, starting to understand that the joke had been on her.

"I can't teleport, but I can disappear."

"You were here there the whole time."

"Yep."

"I hate you," Emily grumbled.

Tristan chuckled as they moved back over to the table.

Emily sighed. "Where was I?"

"Sabvon became nomadic," Tristan replied.

Emily threw her fist out and punched his arm.

"Ouch," he said, rubbing his appendage. "Can I have some of the candy?"

Deb giggled as Emily continued. "Sabvon started new and revisited some of his other villages he founded, but without the goddesses' intervention, man has no one keeping him accountable and he is starting to destroy Valencia. Magic outside of Cybele is dying, and man is turning to science and technology to replace it."

"By this time," Deb added, handing Tristan a chocolate, "The memory of the three goddesses of Valencia are but passages found in some old history books."

"Yeah, it was hard to combat. Try as he might, Sabvon couldn't get people to see the wrong in what they were doing. Clearing forest land to build more housing. Damming rivers to power the mills. They saw technology as good, it made people's lives easier. Then we moved into the age of machines powered by wood and coal. Then they found oil, and liquid fuel like gasoline was born."

"And there goes our air," Deb grumbled.

"Let's not forget electricity," Tristan added.

"No, we can't forget that. Can you imagine our world without it?"

Tristan nodded and the both girls laughed. "Besides Cybele, there are very few places on earth without it. I used to live for my smartphone," Emily said. "Always checking it for messages. Popping online looking to see what people were up to. Now I rarely carry it with me."

"Me too," Tristan sighed.

"I still carry mine," Deb said, pulling it out of her back pocket. "I text my folks once in a while just to let them know I'm still alive."

The three looked blankly out into the room, thinking about life without electricity. Finally Deb asked, "So, what happened to him?"

Emily shrugged her shoulders, "I don't know, it doesn't say. None of the scrolls say anything about his demise, or that of his sister or whatever happened to Yorick."

Deb looked over at her friend. "There is the crypt in the Sacred Valley."

"Yeah, there is that," Emily pondered. "I wonder what we'd find if we dug it up?"

Chapter Five

Emily knelt beside the stone and looked at the elemental symbols decorating the top and sides. In the center was a large paw print. Tristan touched her shoulder and pulled her back from the grave. "There's a powerful spell sealing that tomb."

"We need to get in, how do we break it?"

"Without killing ourselves, I have no idea."

Emily sat on the ground resting her arm on Tegula and pondering their next move. Suddenly, her arm rest disappeared and then reappeared with reinforcements. "What are you guys doing here?" she asked, the two little gnomes she had called Masai and Vulpes.

"We're here to help," Vulpes said, giving Emily a hug.

Emily returned the hug and gave one to Masai as well. "Help doing what?"

"Please move behind that large tree over there," Masai said.

Emily looked alarmed at Tegula, who was walking around the grave site staring at the stone almost as if he was calculating something.

"Tegula!" Emily shouted. "What are you doing?"

Tegula gave her a quick little wave and dropped below the surface. Emily fell back against Tristan as the two remaining gnomes transported them and Deb behind the tree, then disappeared as well. Scrambling to her feet, she peeked around the tree in time to see a burst of light and wall of fire shoot forth from the grave site, blowing the stone slab into the air about twenty feet and knocking

her back about ten. She could feel someone touching her

but couldn't quite get her eyes to open.

Tegula patted her hand and gently talked to her.

"Please be okay," he whispered. "Ptilopsis is going to be

angry when he finds out that I put you in harm's way

again."

"Is she okay?" a voice asked, lost in the dust cloud

behind them.

Deb grabbed Tristan's arm and stared at the stranger

in a hooded cloak moving towards them. "Wow," she said.

"Yeah, double wow," he replied.

Tegula looked up at the gentle soul in a dusty green

robe standing before him. "I think so."

The old man knelt beside Emily and laid his hand on her head. "That should help," he whispered. "Just got the wind knocked out of her, she'll be all right in couple of minutes. As the dust settled, the old man stood and looked around him. "My, I hope all of this wasn't caused by you releasing me?"

There was silence for several minutes before Deb mustered the courage to speak. "This village has been in ruins for thousands of years," she said, stepping forward. "Are you the Beastmaster?"

Scratching his bearded chin, he thought for a moment. "It was a name I used to go by," he said, kneeling back down beside Emily. "A long, long time ago."

"Wow!"

Tristan looked at Deb then back to the old man. "Can someone explain to me what just happened here, how did the stone get moved?"

"Best I can figure out," the old man said. "Your little friends there asked the trees to lift off the stone off. From under the ground, that is."

Tegula and the other two gnomes went to the old man's side. "You are amazing little creatures. Where did you come from?" he asked, studying each one individually.

"Terra," they all piped in. "Ava is the goddess there."

"How intriguing."

"If you're really the son of Adele, that would make her your aunt," Deb said. "Aunt Ava."

The old man scratched his head, and looked around him again. "It sounds like I have a lot of catching up to do. Is there somewhere a little more comfortable we can take your friend?"

Deb looked at Tegula. "Can you move us without Emily's help?"

"No, he can't, but I can," said a voice that surrounded them like the mist swirling at their feet.

Deb saw tears rolling down the old man's face as they were slowly engulfed in fog.

"Cathleena," he whispered. "You've come back to us."

Emily sat on the grassy glade with Tristan, Deb and the gnomes, trying to figure out everything she'd missed.

Inside the marble structure in front of them, they watched Cathleena and the old man talk.

"That's the Beastmaster?" Emily asked, shielding her eyes from the glaring sun to get a better look at the man. "He's not how I imagined. I mean, the statues…"

"Were of him when he was younger," Tristan said, interrupting her. "He's like two thousand years old now."

"You make that sound like I'm ancient," the old man chuckled coming upon them. "Why, my aunt Cathleena is--"

"Let's not get into that," Cathleena said abruptly. "Show him the mark, Emily."

Emily stood and pulled down the collar of her shirt to show him the paw print on her chest.

"Yep," he said, examining the mark, "its Zorrie's, all right."

The three exchanged glances. "Zorrie's?" they said in unison.

"Your dog?" Cathleena laughed.

"Yeah. The spaniel you gave me when I was a kid."

"A dog? I thought it was a wolf's paw print," Emily said in disgust.

"What's wrong with a dog?" the old man asked. "My mother chose that as my sign. That dog and I were inseparable."

"Nothing against your mother, but it's not as cool as a wolf," Deb replied.

"And you are?" he asked sternly.

"Deb. I'm her friend," she said, pointing to Emily.

"And a believer, I sense. And you, wizard?" he said, turning to Tristan.

"How did you know he was a wizard?" Emily asked in surprise.

The old man held his hand up to silence her. "I've been gone awhile, but I know Gifted Ones when I see them."

"Tristan, sir, from the school of magic in Cybele."

The old man's face brightened. "Cybele. It still exists?"

"Yes, sir, there's over two hundred followers at any given time there."

"Followers. Followers of magic?"

"No sir, followers of the goddess," he said nodding to Cathleena.

"Did you know that, Aunty?"

Cathleena shook her head. "No. There's so much I'm still learning from my time away."

"Extraordinary," he said, moving up next to Emily. "And I understand you're in charge of transportation."

Emily pointed to the gnomes, "It's more like they are."

"Ah, the creatures that blew up my tomb."

Tegula, Vulpes and Masai lowered their eyes and bowed to the old man. "We're very sorry," Tegula said. "My ideas never seem to work out the way I think they will."

Cathleena chuckled. "He is called the Young One on Terra, though I believe Emily has given them all special names."

"She calls me Tegula. After a type of sea snail," he said, pointing to his hat which was the shell of such a snail.

"My name is Masai, after the tallest giraffe."

"Oh I see, you are a bit taller than the others," he said, kneeling down next to the gnomes. "Aren't you?"

"And I'm Vulpes, named after a type of fox that's no longer on this world," she said, with a curtsy.

"What do you mean, no longer on this world?"

"It's extinct," Emily said. "All of its kind have died out. There are no more here on Valencia. In fact, a lot of the animals you once knew are gone."

The old man gave Cathleena a startled looked. "Is this the reason I've been awakened?"

Cathleena shrugged. "I do not know. But I'm glad you're here."

He sighed and shook his head. After a moment's thought, he turned to Emily. "I sense you are a lover of animals?"

"I'm a biologist, that's a scientist who studies living organisms in their own environment."

The old man blinked.

"Yes, I love all things of nature," she said with a smile. "Especially animals."

The old man nodded. "But how did you come by that?" he said, pointing to the mark on her chest. "Cathleena believes you're from my line. But truthfully, I do not know of any offspring. Not saying that there couldn't be. I did travel a great deal. And there were quite a few lonely nights when I sought out companionship," he said, thoughtfully.

Emily and the others stared at him as he lost himself in some old memories. She cleared her throat, bringing his thoughts back to the present. "So how would I have gotten this?" she asked.

The old man stared at her, then looked to his aunt. "There are a lot of questions that need answering," he said. "But this one, you're going to have to do."

"Explain."

"The only one I can think of that would put this sign on a baby would be Mother."

Cathleena tried to hide the sudden shock her nephew's words caused her. Putting herself in check, she said, "I leave you, Nephew, in good hands. Watch out for each other." Glancing down at the gnomes she pointed to Vulpes and Masai. "Ava is expecting you two back."

The two gnomes bowed to the goddess and disappeared.

Cathleena started to walk back over to the stairs of the pavilion, and slowly ascended them. Once at the top of the stairs, she stopped and turned back to the group. "Welcome back, Beastmaster," the goddess said, as she started to shimmer and fade. "What message have you for your mother?"

"That I love and miss her," he said, with a sigh. "Very much."

Chapter Six

The Beastmaster circled the statue of himself, studying every little aspect of it. "The jaguar cub I called Ada. I found her injured on the side of the road. Couldn't find her mother, so I brought her here. She stayed with me for over twenty years. The snake was Apep, the eagle was Ziben."

Deb laughed. "You're not very creative with names. They're all Sipen words. Ada means sleek. Apep, slither. Zib-beno, black-feathered."

"You know Sipen?"

Deb looked at him sheepishly. "A little."

Emily laughed. "Just enough to get her into trouble. Tashen and Sipen are used a lot with Biology."

"Biology, the study of living things?"

Emily chuckled, "You remembered."

"Trying. There's so much that has changed here."

Deb nudged the other two and pointed at the small group of people being led by Tristan that were heading their way.

Emily acknowledged Manalia, the village alchemist, with a nod.

"I hear you will no longer need the potion of understanding for the scrolls," she said.

"No," Emily replied, "I have the author right here. I'm hoping to hear all his stories first-hand from now on."

A tall, slender man made his way up to Emily and her companions. Stepping in front of the Beastmaster, he said with a bow, "*Canavarın tebrik ustası. Sizi evinize geri döndürüyoruz. Tanrıya övgü beklemek sonunda bitti.*"

Emily moved to Tristan's side and whispered. "What did he say?"

Tristan shrugged. "I don't speak ancient tongue."

The old man returned the bow. "*Tanrıçayı kutsa, çünkü geri döndü. Yakında gelecek pek çok değişiklik olacak. Cathleena, dünyanın imha edilmesini diliyor. Haydi gelelim sevinçten ve ekmek kıralım.*"

With a chuckle the Beastmaster turned to Deb and Emily, "He said, Greetings, Master of the Beast. We welcome you back to your home. Praise the Goddess, the wait is finally over. And I said, Bless the Goddess, for she has returned as well. Soon, there will be many changes to come. Cathleena wishes the destruction of her world to end. Come let us rejoice and break bread." He laughed again, as he, Deb, and Emily followed the others to the main dining hall. "I think he was testing me. Glad my brain's still working after all those years of sleep."

"Testing you, why?"

Tristan stopped in front of them as they prepared to enter the room. "Because it's a little hard to believe that the prophecy has finally been fulfilled and the Savior has returned after two thousand years." Tristan opened the door and allowed the others to enter first.

The Great Hall was bustling with excitement. Word was spreading like wildfire through the village about the return of the Beastmaster. The foursome exchanged looks, and then followed Tristan to the table at the front of the room. The group who had met them in the courtyard was waiting for them to take their seats before sitting themselves.

Emily and Deb were in awe as they looked around them. It was like being in an old castle with torches on the walls for lights and dozens of candled chandeliers.

"*Üstat*," the slender man said, before being cut off by the old man.

"Let's speak a language that all will be able understand," the old man said. "Interpreting is very tiring."

The man nodded. "I understand, son of Adele."

"I like to know who I'm talking to," said the Beastmaster. "And you are?"

"I am Josiah, the Magistrate of Cybele."

"Outstanding, very pleased that Cybele has survived and," he said, glancing around him. "Prospered."

"I assure you Master, it is as you left it," Josiah said with a swipe of his arms.

The old man chuckled. "Well, not exactly as I left it, I hope. As I recall my quarters was a disaster."

Emily was the only one who noticed the guest of honor sneaking out of his own welcome home party, only hours into the celebration. Following him, she went behind the hanging tapestry at the side of the room and ducked through the hidden passages before the door could shut all the way. Fumbling through the darkened passage, she finally made it out to a clearing on the backside of the compound.

As her eyes adjusted to the light, she watched the old man as he sat down on a large rock and looked out over a small group of swine rooting around a nearby tree. Within minutes all four pigs moved to the side of the Beastmaster, demanding attention.

"They're like puppies," he said, rubbing bellies and scratching behind ears.

Emily remained motionless and silent, not knowing to whom he was talking.

He waved her forward. "I know you're back there, Beastmaster. Come forward."

"You're the Beastmaster, not I," she said timidly, as she sat beside him on the rock.

"True, you're not a master yet, but you will be." He gave her a cheerful pat on the leg, and chuckled. "I can't live forever you know."

He laughed softly for a moment, then he stood he said, "My aunt told me you're very special, and I can sense that. So I ask you, do you want to continue serving your goddess or do you want to return to your old life?"

Emily laughed nervously. "I can't just forget about this place."

The old man held her gaze with his own. "Yes, you can. I can make you forget all about the things that have happened to you in the past two years. Cathleena has granted me that power."

"I don't understand," Emily said, shaken. "Have I done something wrong?"

"No child," he said, touching her arm and sending a calming feeling throughout her body. "You have not." Sensing her discomfort, he changed subjects. "Tell me about the animals."

"What animals?"

"Why, the ones you've saved."

"Oh, okay," she said, calling Tegula to her side.

As Tegula appeared the old man knelt down and touched his shoulder. "Truly a magnificent creature. Where to first?"

"Home. There's a lot there I can show you and it's easier than traveling all over the planet."

The old man wandered around Emily's house, studying and looking at everything from the refrigerator in the kitchen to the radio alarm clock in the bedroom. Plus, he used every form of the word "spectacular" that he could think of.

"Splendid, truly inspiring. What they do with dwellings in the future is wonderful."

Emily moved toward her office area, "At least you got the concept about refrigeration," she laughed. "You should have seen the gnomes trying to figure it out."

"I did?" he asked with a smirk. "I didn't understand a word you said, but it is a truly remarkable contraption."

Emily laughed again and guided him to the map on her wall that listed all the endangered animals that she had removed from Valencia.

After what seemed like an eternity of silence, he finally spoke. "This is all quite disturbing," he said, pointing to the pictures on the map. "All gone, you say."

Emily nodded, "The ones we could save are now on Terra."

"Will you bring them back?"

"Only if we can fix the problem."

"Which is?"

"Arrogant and ignorant humans."

"I see," he said solemnly. "Then I ask you again. Do you want to continue to serve your goddess, or go back to your old way of life?"

"What's wrong with what I'm doing now?" she asked.

"I can't teach the ways of a Beastmaster if you're half in this world and half in the other. Cathleena wants Valencia on the road to mend, and quickly. We are to do whatever is necessary to bring this to pass."

Emily hesitated a moment. "There's no one here for me, I have no family."

"If this means what we think it means, you have me," he said, pointing to the mark on her chest. "And that means you have Cathleena as well."

The old man walked off a large circle around Emily and then joined her in the center. Closing his eyes, he used the natural power of the planet to seek out the animals in the area. Emily could feel the energy of the magic pass through her and surround her. She'd never felt anything like it before in her life.

"They are there," he said, his eyes still closed in concentration. "Call out to them. If one enters the circle I know you have done well."

Emily closed her eyes and tried to think of what kind of animal would be in an area like this. In a short time a picture of a deer popped into her head. To her delight when she opened her eyes there was indeed a doe standing in front of her just a few feet outside the line.

Emily stretched out her hand and tried to coax the beast to her. *Come here little one,* she said, trying to reach the animal with her mind. Of course, it sounded a lot easier than it was proving to be.

"Hear the beast here," he said tapping her head, "And feel it here." He put his finger to her chest. "When you're one with nature, she will talk to you, and you will hear her."

"Are you talking about Cathleena?"

"Cathleena is echoed throughout this world. She is nature, and nature is she. Now back to the deer."

"What about your mother? Was she a part of this world?"

"The lesson today is not about my mother, now back to the deer."

"Please, you said they're my family. I want to understand them."

Heaving a sigh, the old man began. "Each had their own powers, their own strengths, and their own weaknesses. It's how Jabaz created them. None could ever be as powerful as him. Or more powerful than the other."

"He made them flawed?"

The old man nodded. "Yes, I guess you could say that." He placed three rocks in a shape of a triangle then connected them with a line from one to the other. "Nature, Elements, and Humans. The power of Valencia was shared equally by the three. But if you take one away," he said, removing a rock.

"It's like a circuit," she said, after a moment. "The power's still there, but the two remaining sisters couldn't use it as efficiently as when there was three." Emily saw the bewildered look on his face, then added. "Why didn't

Jabaz make it so that the two would be able to go on without the third?"

"I doubt it ever crossed his mind."

Emily thought for a moment then said. "Is Cathleena going to be able to do this by herself? She's nature, can she tap into the other powers?"

"She is determined to do so," he said, closing his eyes again. "Now let's see if you are as determined as she to reach your goal. Your deer has wandered off. Let us see if you can call her back to you."

Chapter Seven

For a brief moment Cathleena rested her hand on the small oak tree outside the entrance to the underworld, before stepping under the crumbling stoned archway known as Anxiety and Grief and going inside. Moving down the corridor, she passed under many more such arches. There was Fear, and Disease, farther down from those was Hunger, and farther down yet, Agony and Death.

This was not the kind of family reunion she would have wished for. As she entered a rather large cavern she noticed the mist rising up from the floor. As it rose, the figure of a woman in a blood red gown began to emerge. Behind her, also rising with the mist, was a woman with flaming red hair dressed in white hooded robes. Once they'd completely materialized, a small breeze blew through the cavern and swept the remaining wisps of fog away.

"I was surprised to hear that you were back on Valencia," Nia said, moving closer to her daughter. "But not surprised that you are here without your father's permission."

Cathleena lowered her head slightly, and spoke. "Thank you for bringing Adele to me, Mother."

Nia walked slowly around her youngest daughter, eyeing her suspiciously. "Are you going to tell me why you are here?"

"If I don't, and Father asks, then you have nothing to fear."

Nia studied her a moment, then placed a hand on her shoulder. "You are not your sister, Cathleena. This deception does not suit you."

"All right, Mother, I want to save our world. I want to right the wrong that I allowed to happen in my weakness and absences. And I have spoken to Father," she said, facing her mother. "He has forsaken Valencia and all upon it. He will neither help nor hinder me. As he put it, 'Valencia's fate has been left to me.'"

Adele stepped around her mother and moved in front of her sister. Cathleena embraced her, not wanting to extinguish the hold. "Sabvon is with me, and he sends his love," she said stepping back and conjuring up his image between them.

Tears poured down Adele's face as she gazed upon her son's wizened face. "On my, he has not aged well, has he?"

"His body may look frail, but he is of strong spirit."

"He was to join us," Nia said, venomously. "That was promised when you arrived."

"Obviously Mother, it's not his time yet," Adele said, and then turned to Cathleena. "You didn't come here just to tell me he was alive and with you. Why did you come?'

Cathleena conjured up Emily and pointed to the mark she bore on her chest. "It's Sabvon's mark, but he says he didn't put it on her. Did you?"

Adele closed her eyes as her mother roared with laughter behind her. "This is the child," Nia said. "The one you sent back into its mother's womb after I brought it here because it had died. See what happens when you try to recruit help down here?" Nia said to Cathleena. "She has no life essence now, because she bestowed it on that child to give it back to its mother that day."

Cathleena stood dumbfounded.

"You know the rules, Daughter. Do not venture past the arches, or you will be forever stuck between two worlds." With that, Nia disappeared in a flash of light.

"What did you do?" Cathleena asked sorrowfully.

"I made it so I wouldn't be stuck for eternity down here with Mother, that's all. Now, like other mortals, I will fade slowly into nothingness. It's already happened to my beloved Octavian, and he's the whole reason I came down here in the first place."

"Is the girl of Sabvon's line?"

"No, Aurelia's." Adele signaled her sister to follow. "Upon death, a soul waits at the entrance of the underworld for our mother to pass sentence based on their deeds during their previous life. It's there that she decides to send them into the Dark Void of Despair or to send them on to the Euphoric Meadows." Adele stopped at the entrance way that led up to the surface. "I used to stand here from time to time to watch over the people of the world. I still have followers, did you know that?"

Cathleena shook her head.

"People who are sick or dying asking for comfort. Mothers still call out to me and ask me to bless their unborn children. For some time, I had been watching a young mother who was a descendant of Aurelia's. She was unable to feel her child move anymore. I ran to Nia to ask her to allow me go out to help, but when I arrived she was already holding the baby. She placed it in my arms and told me to take it to Euphoric Meadows. But instead, behind her back, I took it to the outside world and breathed the rest of my life force into it and placed it back into its mother womb. Death wasn't as bad as I had imagined," Adele said, staring out into the sunshine. "In fact, it's rather peaceful. When I awoke, I was standing outside the entrance there, waiting with the rest of the souls for Mother's judgement."

Adele turned and spotted a tear moving slowly down Cathleena's cheek. "My only regret is that I can no longer hear the voices of our people. But I can bring them some comfort once they arrive here, and that I'll do for as long as I can. The rest, I fear, is up to you now, dear Sister. I do not remember marking the child, perhaps I was hoping that Sabvon or Aurelia would find her someday, but she is indeed the one I saved."

"Aurelia, she's not here?"

Adele shook her head, "That is why Mother is so angry with me. Both my children seemed to have somehow cheated death." Adele grabbed her sister's arms and met her gaze. "Tell me, what is the child like?"

"Emily is so much like Sabvon. Compassionate, but fearless, her love for animals is strong. I thought for sure she was from his line."

"You never got to know Aurelia, Sister. She definitely a child of nature, so much like her brother, but different. I know you would have loved her."

"I'm sorry about your mother," Emily said, as she watched the old man settle down heavily in his chair. The news he had brought back from his Aunt Cathleena was intriguing, but also painful for the few that were involved.

"I'm not," he said, patting her hand. "It's exactly what I'd expect from her. And look at you. It warms this old heart knowing that she's a part of you. And besides, fading away into nothingness doesn't sound like that bad of a thing."

"Hey, old man," Emily teased. "Don't get any funny ideas on leaving us, we just got you back."

"For what?"

Emily looked startled and looked from one to the other of her friends, then back to the old man. "You're supposed to help us fix the world."

"How?"

"How am I supposed to know? You're the savior."

"I got the name when I led a hundred battered, starving, homeless individuals across the Tehys marsh and up the Upper Maygar River, and into the Old forest of Dane, defeated the shadows and built Cybele, where they were given hope of a semi-normal life. How am I supposed to help this time? I don't know your world. What is it that we need to do to save it?"

"Stop man from destroying it, for one," Emily said angrily.

"So I say again, how?"

Emily sat down at the table next to him. Tristan and Deb joined them. "I don't know," she said, slumping her shoulders. "To save the animals, I had to take them away."

"But it didn't stop the problem?"

"No. The rivers are still dammed, and the forests are still being cut down. The air, land, and water are all polluted. And man is still exploiting the animals that we share this world with."

The old man rubbed his bearded chin then looked over at her. "Who's damming up the rivers?"

"Power companies."

Tegula suddenly appeared and moved over to Emily's side. At first she wasn't sure why he was there, but then guessed that the Beastmaster somehow called him.

"Are you two coming?" he asked Deb and Tristan. "We're going to go look at a power company."

Deb laughed as she held Tristan and the old man's hand. "Where to, Em?"

Emily shrugged. "Only been to the Upper Maygar Dam, guess we'll start there."

"Reaches Resources," Tristan said, reaching for Emily's hand. "Wow, we're going to take on the big guy."

Emily shrugged. "Why not?"

Emily could tell by the look on the old man's face that he was overwhelmed by what he was seeing around him. The noise was deafening, but before she could suggest that they move he waved his hand, stopping all motion of the water pouring through the spillways.

"Wow," Deb exclaimed. "That was cool."

"Couldn't hear a thing," he said, clearing his ears. "Now. What is this monstrosity?"

"This is what they call a dam," Emily said, then continued by describing the basic function and how it generated power. "The problem is that it stops fish like salmon from returning to their spawning grounds upstream. If they can't spawn, there are no further generations. Without salmon, animals like the Northern

Strait Orcas starve. They're one of the animals I moved to Terra."

"That's very sad. But an easy fix."

"The only way to fix it is to remove the dam. But none have ever been removed. Companies like Reaches Resources depend on them to make the electricity that they sell to the people to heat their homes and run their appliances."

"Let me understand something. The power created by this thing is not given to the people freely?"

"No, they have to pay for it."

The old man whispered something to Tegula, and the whole group appeared at the river's edge. "Then it's decided."

Before their eyes, the cement structure disappeared and the river and surrounding area went back to the way it was before the dam had been built.

"Awesome!" Deb yelled.

"Now, that's magic," Tristan exclaimed.

Emily looked at each of her friends with a shocked look on her face. "Do you know what you've done?" she snapped, turning to the Beastmaster.

"I solved the problem."

"You created another. People are going to be without power now."

"I do not understand, you said the rivers being dammed was a problem, so I removed it."

Emily looked around, trying to comprehend everything that was happening. "Yes, the dam was a problem, but now we're going to have people with no heat, lighting, or any way to cook their food."

"I see," said the old man, replacing the cement structure with another wave of his hand. "So, we have a problem that cannot be fixed without affecting the commoners."

The old man watched as the three young people argued amongst themselves. "Let him do it. It'll send a message," Tristan said, angrily. "It's what we talked about before. To fix our planet, people are going to have to learn to live without power."

"I agree," Deb piped in. "Cybele did it, the rest of the world can do it too."

Emily shook her head. "We're letting our anger blind us. Are we killers? Because if we go around removing all the dams, a lot of people are going to die. There has to be another way," she said starting to pace.

After a moment of silence. "She's right," Tristan said, letting out a calming breath. "The people in Cybele can live without power because they've gone back to the old ways, and they have magic."

Emily looked over at the dam.

"You've got that look on your face. What are you thinking?" Deb said, moving up next to her.

"I think it's time to get the word out," Emily said, turning to the group. "We'll start with the power companies. Then we'll move on to the forest industries, and so on, and so on. We're going to warn the people first, then we'll start turning off the power."

"Oh. Oh!" Deb said raising her hand and jumping. "Let me."

"Do what?" Emily asked.

"Hold a press conference."

"I think we all need to be there, Deb."

"I want to go to my Dad's university. I think the first one should be there."

"Why?"

"Because there is nothing like having a bunch of college kids backing your cause."

Chapter Eight

The plant foreman stood by the closed door a moment, sucked in a deep breath, and then rapped his knuckles against the dark oak panel.

"Yes?" a deep voice reverberated through the door.

"It's me, Mr. Yardan. Peter Hopkins."

"Enter."

Turning the knob, he opened the door just wide enough for him to squeeze through and then closed it quickly behind him. Across the room from him with only a desk lamp to light the room, the CEO of Reaches Resources, a silver haired man who looked to be in his early sixties, sat behind the large dark walnut desk.

"What is it, Hopkins?" the older man asked in an unwelcoming tone. "And make it quick," he said looking up from his ledger. "I don't have all day."

"We had an occurrence at one of the dams today," Hopkins said, wringing his hands nervously.

"You've taken care of it, I assume?" the man behind the desk asked, before returning to his ledgers.

"Yes sir, I mean, it kinda took care of itself, sir."

"Then why are bothering me, Hopkins?"

"We don't know what caused it, sir. The dam went offline, then before we could get a crew out there to see what had happened, it came back on."

Rocking back in his chair, the man behind the desk glared across the room at the foreman. Hopkins backed up against the door as the man's eyes began to glow red from within the shadows where he sat.

"There's a tape, sir. The crew recovered the security tape."

"And?"

"Before the dam went off line there was a small group of people up on the parapet. Then they... well, they just disappeared."

"Interesting, I would like to see this tape."

"Yes, sir," Hopkins said, slowly making his way around the desk to the computer in the middle. After punching in a code, he brought up the security tape from the dam that morning and showed it to his boss.

Hopkins had steeled himself for the worst, but the laughter that came out of him boss's mouth scared him more than the angry rant he was expecting.

"My word. It seems my cousin has returned," the CEO chuckled. "It's too bad, when I sealed him in his grave all those years ago, I had hoped never to see him again."

Hopkins trembled as he backed slowly toward the door. "If that will be all sir, I'll be returning to the plant?" he said, fumbling for the doorknob.

Yardan continued the wicked laughing as he watched the video again and again. "Of course, go," he said. Absentmindedly he waved his hand and sent his foreman flying through the closed door, killing him instantly. With the sound of the crash he looked up from the tape, perturbed. He moved away from his desk to the shattered door and crumbled body of the foreman. He studied the scene for a moment and then shook his head in frustration. With another wave of his hand the door became whole again and the body disappeared. "I really must pay attention to what I'm doing. I lose more good help that way."

They had both attended the University of Stell, so both knew exactly where to draw the biggest crowd. Moving down to the front doors of the student activities center, Emily handed Deb a megaphone she often used for her own outdoor speeches, and waited for classes to let out.

Eyeing the Beastmaster, Emily had to chuckle at his inquisitive curiosity. With eyes full of wonder he wandered around, taking in the sights of what they had told him was a gigantic place of learning.

Deb clicked on the megaphone and climbed to the middle of the steps leading into the dining hall as the students started emptying the other building and headed towards her. "She has returned!" she yelled. "And she is pissed. Mankind has laid his destructive hand on her beloved planet, and now she seeks restitution. Who, you ask?" she said, pointing at a young man who had stopped in front of her. "Cathleena! Youngest of the three, Goddess of Valencia, has returned to our world and she is not happy with what she has seen. She's already removed from our planet her beloved animals we humans had put on the brink of extinction." Deb began to pace and became more animated as the crowd grew. "No longer will you find Elephants or Rhinos on the Farwest plains, or Armadillos and Black Bears in Panthalassa. They're gone, taken away from our planet so that their senseless slaughter would stop."

The crowed was getting bigger, Emily and Deb had picked the perfect time to hold the demonstration. Lunchtime. Deb moved farther up onto the steps so that the people in back could see her. "They're gone!" she shouted again. "All of them. Even our Northern Strait Orcas that used to swim right off our coast," she said pointing to the west. "Not even twenty miles from here. They, are, gone! Cathleena has taken them all away because mankind was too arrogant or ignorant to know that we are destroying our planet, and by doing so, killing the creatures that we share Valencia with."

Emily stepped up next to Deb. "Security's coming up the walk," she whispered. "And I don't know if you noticed, but we're being filmed. I think it's time to make a grand exit." Taking the megaphone from Deb, she said, "Some of you may know me. My name is Emily Dickens. I'm a conservationist and have spoken out for years against the destruction of our world's resources and its wildlife. I wanted to let you know how desperate this situation is. Cathleena wants her world back the way it was before she left. Help stop the destruction of our world and return it to its glorious self, or suffer the consequences."

"Hey, look there's my dad," Deb told Emily as she pointed to a man in the back.

Emily called Tegula to her side, joined hands with the others, and before the first security officer could make it through the crowd and up the steps, the group disappeared.

Emily paced on the boat dock as Deb talked on the phone. She couldn't hear everything, but what she did hear wasn't good. The group had been taken to Blue Water Cove where Tristan, Tegula and the Beastmaster were entertaining themselves with the surrounding wildlife. Emily always loved coming here. The serenity of the place often calmed her troubled soul. But today, there was no relief from her strenuous lifestyle by enjoying the presence of her beloved manatees, only concern for Mr. Palmer, Deb's father. Finally, after about twenty minutes Deb hung up the phone and looked over at her friend.

"Well?" Emily said, stepping up next to her.

"Umm, the government guys had him, but they let him go after questioning him for a couple of hours. Umm… we've been labeled as terrorists because of the dam incident."

"Deb," Emily nudged her, pointing at the men approaching from the road. Within seconds, both Tristan and the Beastmaster were surrounded by gun-wielding officers from the government.

The order 'don't move' was shouted at the two, sending Tristan into his disappearing act. Surprised, the old man stood alone and looked around him for his companion.

"What the—Where did he go?" one of the officers demanded, pointing his gun at the old man.

Puzzled he answered. "I don't know."

"Put your hands up and get down on the ground."

"Which am I supposed to do first? Because at my age, I can't do both at the same time."

The officer cursed and physically shoved the Beastmaster to the ground. "Here you old fart, I'll help you."

"I was warned that man had become more arrogant," the Beastmaster said, anger filling his eyes as he pushed himself off the ground and floated into the air in front of the startled group. Lifting his arms out from his sides, he sent hundreds of sparrow-sized birds darting at the man who had assaulted him. Raising his palms up, he sent another onslaught of bigger birds in an aerial attack at the rest of group, then another, and another, forcing the armed men and women back up the road toward their vehicles.

Tristan made his way to Emily and Deb on the dock and reappeared beside them as they watched in awe while the Beastmaster battled the government troops. Just when they thought that he had sent them running for home, one of the officers fired his gun five times at him.

The Beastmaster stood with his hand out in front of him. Inches from his palm, suspended in the air, were the five bullets.

*"**I am Sabvon, son of the Goddess Adele**. My grandfather, creator of all things, made this world. You cannot kill me with your puny weapons, human,"* his voice echoed around and through them. A bright light started to glow from beneath him, and then around him, and the ground started to tremble.

Some of the officers contemplated firing their own weapons until the earth beneath them started shaking, tossing them around like rag dolls. And then if that hadn't been bad enough, once the ground stopped moving, out of nowhere they became surrounded by hundreds of wetlands creatures. Snakes, alligators, cougars, boars, beavers, otters, bears, and even a few deer started chasing the men and women back to their cars and then up the road leading out of the glades.

"Wow!" Deb shouted, stomping her feet and laughing.

"Dang!" Tristan yelled, "Did you see that?"

For some unknown reason, Emily started to move away from the others and walked over to the old man. She could sense the unity of the creatures that were moving around him, all with the single purpose of protecting him. Kneeling down on one knee, she closed her eyes and reached out with her mind and her hand and sent a mental messages of friendship and love to all the agitated animals meandering about.

After a moment, she could hear him chuckling. "Well done, my young apprentice. You will be a master of the beast soon enough."

Emily felt a nudge on her left shoulder, and a bump on her right hip, and a bony armored snout pushing against her outstretched hand. Opening her eyes, she was a little startled to see a 12 foot alligator lying in front of her with his nose resting on her hand, and then realized that a rather large male cougar was rubbing against her like a domestic house cat, and that the bumping on her hip was a cute little otter trying to get her cell phone out of her back pocket. She stood up slowly and looked over at her friends and smiled. With her hand resting on the cougar's shoulder she said, "I could get used to this."

Turning off the news, Mr. Yardan sat back in the chair and rubbed his chin thoughtfully. "So that's it. She's returned and is unhappy with what we've done with the place in her absence."

"Why would she come back?" his wife asked, handing him a cup of tea. "I thought they gave up on the place. It was too much for them to handle, you said."

"Grandfather sent them away, truth be known. I think Cathleena would had stayed out of loyalty for your mother and brother. It was Zorine's overpowering personality that condemned them both."

"What are we going to do?"

"Do? Yes, this could become annoying. I'll have to think more on the issue."

"I don't like it."

"Why are you bothered? Could it be the fact that your brother is back as well?"

She ignored her husband's taunt and returned to the watering of her plants. As she did so, she looked at the wrinkles and age spots on her hands. "When are we going to do the change? I want to be young and beautiful and wear glamorous things again. I hate being old," she said in disgust. "You promised me that I'd never grow old."

"I promised you eternal life, my dear Aurelia, not eternal youth. Growing old is all a part of the vizard. But you're right, my dear," he said as he stood. "With Sabvon and his group going after power companies, this could become a bigger problem for us. I'll try to find a buyer for Reaches Resources and look into getting us new identities and a new life somewhere else." He stopped as he started to leave the room, then turned to her and added, "I heard rumor that the shuttle program was finally coming back

after that disastrous launch a while back. Maybe it's time

for me get back into petroleum. They'll be needing fuel for

their rockets soon."

Chapter Nine

Emily, Deb and her parents stood on the path that led into the city of Cybele, arguing. It was clear that Mr. and Mrs. Palmer did not like being whisked away, even though their house had been surrounded by government troops for the past two days, waiting for their fanatic child to make contact with them.

"I'm sorry, I really am, but we had to get you out of there." Deb looked to see Tristan approaching with the old man. "We'll talk more later. But you remember that big surprise I told you about? Well, this is it. Mom, Dad, this is the Beastmaster. The one who got everyone into a frenzy by his antics at the dam and the park."

The old man scowled at Deb. "Both, cases of misunderstanding," he said, with a huff.

Deb laughed. "Beastmaster, these are my parents, Linda and Stan Palmer. They are what people call archaeologists. They study human history and they're experts on mythology and have a fascination with our world's Deities. In fact, my dad did a whole thesis on you and your mother."

The Beastmaster bowed to Deb's parents. "Anlıyorum, Eskiçağ dili konuşabiliyormusun?"

Deb's father looked startled, and then nodded. "Biraz."

"Adele'nin oğlu Sabvon'um. Cybele'ye hoş geldiniz," the old man said, gesturing around them.

"Teşekkür ederim. Burada olmaktan çok heyecanlıyız."

"He is the One," Deb's mother said in awe, grabbing her husband's arm in her excitment. Looking around her she asked. "Annen burada mı?"

The Beastmaster shook his head sadly. "Yok hayır."

"It would be really nice if someone would let the rest of us know what's going on," Emily said, crossing her arms in front of her chest and staring at the old man. "Not all of us can speak the old language."

"My apologies, my young apprentice. I was just welcoming Linda and Stan to Cybele. And Linda was asking about my mother. Come, let us show these people their new home."

Deb's mother caught her daughter's arm, and pulled her to a stop. "What does he mean by our 'new home'? We can't stay here permanently."

Deb sighed. "Right now, this is the safest place for you. Come on, we can talk while we walk. I made sure your quarters are close to mine."

Emily, Tristan and the Beastmaster sat in the eatery going over plans for their next step when Deb and her parents joined them for lunch.

"I'm afraid we don't have any money to pay for this," Stan said, accepting a plate of bread and cheese and a cup of water.

"You are our guests," the old man said. "Eat and rest. The real work is yet to begin."

"What does that mean exactly?" Linda asked, accepting her own food and drink.

"From what we've heard from the outside world, no one is taking us seriously," Emily said sadly. "It's time for action. Cathleena says 'that no food shall come from the ocean until they start cleaning it up.' So…We're going to go and pass on her message. And it's also time we went and talked to Parliament."

"What can we do?" Stan asked.

"You and the fine people of Cybele are going to spread the word of Cathleena's return. We've got to get people to understand that things are going to be changing and it's not going to be necessarily to their liking. You'll be working with the magistrate of Cybele, Josiah, on this," the old man said. "Tristan and his fellow magic users will start figuring out ways to repair those things on Valencia that are beyond man's capability."

"Like?" Tristan asked.

"Like the ice caps that used to cover the northern and southern tips of our world. But those we may leave until last. Weather changes right now would put people more on edge."

"What about the trash?" Emily said. "It's everywhere. On land, in the oceans and rivers. All man knows how to do with the garbage that he's created is to move it from one place to another or bury it. Here in Cybele you got rid of it?"

"It's returned to the elements from which it's made." Tristan replied then chuckled. "Okay, you collect it and I'll send a group around to get rid of it. But mind you, it takes a lot of energy to reduce garbage to nothing. We have two masters and only ten apprentices at the school."

"I'll talk to the masters and see what I can do to help them in this task," the old man said, rising to his feet. "We may have to rely on Valencia itself to remove some of the refuse. But for now, Emily is going to take me down to the docks for some sight-seeing."

"I am?"

He nodded. "You are."

"Are you serious?" Emily asked, standing on the side of the dock. "Why don't we just take a boat?"

"Why put your trust in a man-made object and not one of Cathleena's creatures? Here they come, this will be fun."

Emily looked at the pod of grey whales coming towards them. "Fun? Is that everything to you?"

The old man stepped down onto the back of the closest whale. "If you're not having fun when dealing with the creatures of our world, then you're doing something wrong. Watch out, that one is a little too..."

Emily went to climb on to the back of the whale closest to her, but the animal moved and she slipped into the water.

"I was going to say too young," the Beastmaster said magically lifting her out of the water and placing her on the back of an older, bigger whale. "You can tell the littler one is excited and wants to play. I'm sure he didn't mean you any harm."

Emily looked over at the old man miserably in her heavy, waterlogged clothing. "Sorry, I guess I should have noticed."

With a wave of his hand she was dried off and seated safely on the back of the whale before the pod started moving. Emily couldn't help but laugh at the sight in front of her. The Beastmaster remained standing as if riding a surfboard. She hadn't any idea where they were going until she noticed several fishing vessels ahead them, heading out to sea.

Like some kind of mythical legend riding out of the pages of history on his powerful steed, the Beastmaster pulled up alongside the first ship with his whale. Between the shouts and the sound of ships motors, the old man couldn't hear a thing. With a wave of his hand, the ships stopped and noise silenced. The ship's crew stood staring dumbfounded at the little old man standing beside them.

"Turn back," he said, his voice booming all around them. "There is nothing out here for you, for Cathleena, Goddess of Valencia says 'No food shall come from her oceans until man starts putting forth the effort to clean them.'"

The crew from the ship started to laugh, hrowing gestures and profanity at the old man.

"Did you not hear me?" he asked calmly.

Again, the vulgar language erupted from the deck.

Out all of the men on board, only one wore a hat and no rain gear. Targeting him, the Beastmaster magically lifted the man off the deck and brought him to the back of the whale with him. "Did you hear what I told you?" the old man asked again.

The captain stood shaking with a look of terror on his face, and even from where she was sitting Emily could tell that the man had peed his pants. The Beastmaster spoke again, forcing the other to look him in the eye. "I am the son of Adele, and my aunt the Goddess Cathleena has given me a message for all mankind to hear. 'No food shall come from her oceans until man starts putting forth the effort to clean them.' Do you understand what I'm telling you?"

The captain nodded, and the old man placed him back on the deck of his ship. Yelling out the order to get under way, the frightened man ran into the ship's cabin and locked the door.

"One down, two to go. Do you want to handle the next one?" he asked, Emily.

Tristan stood next to Emily at one end of the boat ramp, poking a stick at the pile of garbage that had been pulled ashore by the fishing fleet that she and the old man had encountered. On the dock above them, the Beastmaster talked with a wizard named Davidson, one of the masters from the school of magic, and two of his apprentices.

"Man, this stuff smells."

Emily wrinkled her nose. "It's so bad in the water."

"So finish what you were saying, what about the other two ships?"

"I'm a little more diplomatic," she said, looking over her shoulder. "But I think we finally got our message across to the other captains."

"And the trash?"

"Added bounce. We spotted it on our way back in, and asked the fishermen, nicely, to haul it to shore for us."

"Nicely, huh?"

"He doesn't like messing around."

Tristan sighed. "I've never seen this much garbage outside a dump before in my life. And I lived in Topios. Makes me sick to think this was just floating around in the water out there."

"There's a lot more," Emily said sadly. "Come on, I think they're ready to get started."

Tristan joined the other magic users and started what ended up to be a three-hour process of breaking down all the trash that had been collected into the elements it had originally come from, and making them vanish.

"It's actually quite boring," the old man said, guiding Emily to the side with him. "I've got a much better plan on how to end our day."

Emily suddenly felt a familiar little hand on her thigh, and before she could ask they left the docks.

Perched above the picturesque Maygar Valley with westerly views of the Hamur lowlands, the beautiful young woman walked through the glamorous living room of her new home and onto the deck where Mr. Yates was busy on the phone. Handing her husband a glass of wine, she moved over to the railing and looked out at their million dollar view, and of course her beautiful orchards that lined the property.

"I love it when we start anew," she said, sucking in a deep breath of air. "Don't you, darling?" With a wave of her hands the apple tree in front of her grew a couple of more inches, bringing a smile to her face.

Mr. Yates held up a finger and continued his conversation. "Excellent. I'll be in Monday first thing in the morning to finish the paperwork. Of course the price was reasonable, if it wasn't I wouldn't have paid it. Don't worry Mr. Barker, I'm quite happy with my purchase."

Giving him a kiss on his cheek, she took the phone and placed it on the table. "So are you going to tell me what happened?"

"It's fairly simple my dear," he said, taking a sip of his wine. "To get back into petroleum I needed a company to make it. Yesterday, I purchased a small company that was on the verge of bankruptcy. Next week I'll have my new crew at Deberk Fuel start revamping everything so that we can start producing rocket fuel for the shuttle program. I was also looking into getting a military deal for my petroleum, but found another company that stood in my way, that's been fixed, although it seems the CEO has recently come up missing along with billions of dollars of his company's money. Everything is fitting into place nicely." He turned to her and raised a brow. "And may I add," he said taking her hand. "You look fabulous." He put his arms around her, bent her back and kissed her softly.

As he released her, she fanned herself wildly. "If only you could show me such passion more than once every forty years."

"Come now," he said, tipping back his glass and finishing his drink. "If you wanted a partner that worshiped the ground you walked on, you should have stayed with that headmaster fellow, Dominic?"

"You know quite well that could not be," she said, turning back to the rail.

"Ah, yes, human, was he not? And that child from your union, whatever happened to him? Did he ever learn that his mother was Adele's daughter? Or was your mother forgotten by then?"

"Stop it. Why must you always taunt me by bringing up the past, I have been faithful to you for over a millennium now."

Yates chuckled and set his wine glass down. "Yes dear, you have, and that's the only reason why I've kept you around."

Chapter Ten

Emily looked around her. Tegula had brought her to a place that was unfamiliar to her. "Where are we?" she asked, turning to the old man.

"Cenaze, or in your words, Eden." He answered as they looked around at the beautiful garden full of trees and wildflowers. "We're not far from where I grew up. The pavilion is up on the other side of that hill. I used to play here as a child," he sighed. "Cathleena and I were the only ones who would ever come here. She and I would spend days, running through the fields, climbing the trees. Well, she would watch me, I don't actually remember her climbing any trees."

"The Garden of Eden?" Emily said sarcastically.

"You laugh, why? Another myth?"

Emily bit her bottom lip.

The old man stepped out into the field running his hand over the top of the flowers. "This is the only place on Valencia now that has every plant that my grandfather ever created. I want to take some of the saplings and seeds from the plants that are no longer on Valencia back to the surface to grow new forest, wetlands, and prairies."

"Okay, so how are we going to do that?"

"We are going to let them do that." The old man gestured to the group of gnomes moving in and out of the field in front of them. "They are much better suited for this than we are."

Emily sat down and laughed as she got swarmed by all her old friends, Vulpes, Ptilopsis, Chelonia, Masai, and even Sirenia was there, all talking a mile a minute, and all with dozens of stories to tell her about the animals from Valencia that they were taking care of for her back on Terra.

"They all truly miss you," she heard a voice say from behind her.

Spinning around, she smiled and got to her feet. Emily greeted the young goddess and started talking to her like some kind of old schoolmate. The old man shook his head in disbelief. Glancing to the side, he spotted Cathleena walking through the field of flowers, running her hands over the tops just as he had done a short time before.

"Well, there is no keeping secrets from you, is there?" he whispered to his aunt as she came up alongside him. "I wanted this to be a surprise."

"I am surprised and very grateful. But for the next time, if you wish me not to learn of one of your plans, don't tell Ava."

"I knew of no other way to recruit the gnomes. I'm a little too old to go sowing fields and planting forests."

Cathleena looked at her nephew with concern. "I know this has been taking its toll?"

"I will do what needs to be done, Aunty. Do not worry about me."

"I do worry though." Cathleena sighed. "At least let me help you." Resting her hand on the old man's shoulder, she removed the pain from his joints and fatigue from his muscles and sent a sense of well-being all throughout his body.

The pair watched as the gnomes moved busily around the field and forest collecting things and disappearing, then reappearing and collecting more.

"There is something you need to know," Cathleena said, glancing his way. "There's magic being used again in the world."

"There's are students from the school in Cybele working on trash removal by Stell."

"No, dear Nephew, this is different. This magical signature is not human." She held his gaze and continued, "At first I didn't think anything about it, I assumed it was you. But then I noticed it the other day and realized it couldn't be you. This one has also been marked with death. There is only one demi-god that I know who carries such a mark. One for whom you yourself killed."

"Yorick, so you found him?" The old man lowered his gaze and thought for a moment. "I'd ask his help, but he was never a true fan of yours. Though there was a time he thought of more than himself. He did start the school of magic in Cybele."

"Why is it that you two get to travel the Tegula express and I have to drudge along the highways and byways of our beloved Valencia to get where I want to go?" Deb asked, greeting her at their makeshift camp.

Emily gave Deb a hug, while Tristan said hello to the others sitting around the fire. "Can't talk to a lot of people, popping in and out like we do. How goes the quest, are people receptive to the news?"

"No," Stan said, joining his daughter and her friend. "We've been spit on, had rotten fruit thrown at us, been chased away by dogs, and a few of us have even been stoned. And I'm not talking about smoking Cannabis."

"Oh, no!" Emily said with a look of alarm. "Is everyone all right?"

"Mostly contusions, scrapes, and cuts," Linda, Deb's mother said, joining them. "But Keven over there suffered a broken arm. We set it the best we could, but he really should get some 'real' medical attention."

"You should have called for help."

"Funny you should mention that," Stan said, circling beside her. "We live in a world of technology, and yet not a single person in this group that you sent us off with owns a working phone. Except for Linda and I of course, but wait, we were whisked away from our home without a single moment to collect any of our valuables, like maybe our cell phones that we could have used to call for help."

"He's a little angry right now," Deb said apologetically.

"Understandably," Emily said sadly.

"What happened to your phone?"

Deb shrugged. "Lost it somewhere."

"It's a good thing we came when we did," Tristan said holding a bag up in his hand. "We brought you something to help you out."

"Magical Amulets," Emily said.

"Amulets?" Deb asked.

Tristan started passing out the bag's contents. "There's amulets for protection, amulets of summoning, amulets for healing…"

"Got any cell phones in that bag?" Stan asked.

Tristan shook his head. "No sir, sorry, I didn't even think about grabbing one."

"Me neither. But I'll see about getting you some. Until then, these amulets that Tristan brought you will help a little. While he's going over how they work, I'll take Keven back to Cybele and have that arm of his checked out."

Deb went with Emily over to where Keven was gathering his things. "We had one bad day," she said, as they walked. "For the most part, people just ignore us."

"What can I do to help?"

"Have any miracles hidden up your sleeve? Because that's what we need. Very few people even remember that there were goddesses here at one time, and having one returned doesn't seem to matter. We've talked to a lot of people, at malls, and at schools, we've been on the news, and in the papers. No one listens, no one cares," Deb sighed. "We'll keep going, but it's really hard to tell anyone anything when no one's listening."

"Have you reestablished any of the old sites?"

"Josiah took a group to Punasia to see if he could get it up and running, and self-sustaining again. And Dad talked some of his colleagues from work into checking out Sacred Valley. Because of its historical value, they're not sure about rebuilding, but may find a place off-site to start another colony."

"I'll see what I can do about getting people to start listening to you guys."

Emily thought for a moment, feeling Tegula up next to her, she put her hand on Keven's back, and said to her friend before they left, "Be safe. I'll send you some phones."

Timing was everything. Emily was really good at knowing when the best time to make a statement would be, and that was first thing in the morning of the opening day of the Western Continental Parliament, which was basically an assemblage of nobility, clergy, and commons that formed the main legislative body of Valencia's western regions.

In the midst of all the shouting and confusion, Emily and the old man moved up to the podium where the Speaker of Parliament, a white-haired man in his early sixties, was going over the day's agenda. The Beastmaster waved his hand quieting all the angry and loud voices. "Cathleena has returned," Emily said, stepping in front of the mic. "And she has demands."

Out of the corner of her eye she saw a security guard draw his weapon, only to have it and all weapons in the room magically taken away by the old man. "It would be best to hear us out," she said, looking over at the guard. "Beside me is the son of Adele, a demi-god with powers beyond comprehension." The guards tried to move closer to the pair at the podium, but became frozen in place with a swipe of the old man's other hand. "This really is silly," she said turning to the Speaker. "Tell them to sit down and hear us out. We'll deliver our message and then we'll leave. Okay?"

The Speaker eyed her for a moment, and then leaned toward the mic. After finding his voice he said, "You heard her. Sit down everyone. Let's hear them out."

Emily stepped past him again to the mic. "Like I said, Cathleena has returned. For those of you who don't remember our planet's history, Cathleena was the youngest of three goddesses who ruled over Valencia thousands of years ago. Since the goddesses' departure, we (mankind) have put our planet along with its plants and animals on the brink of extinction."

Emily watched as the people in front of her tried to complain with no voices. She laughed. "You are a funny bunch. Okay listen. First thing, the oceans need to be cleaned up before she'll allow us to fish again. Secondly, the dams are coming off the rivers, so if you still want your microwave and computers at home to work you'll need to find other sources of power, clean power that won't damage the environment. I'd focus more on wind or solar if I were you. Thirdly, deforestation and the destruction of our wetlands is to stop, and man needs to replant and repair what he's taken down or altered. Fourthly, Cathleena will not stand for senseless killing of animals anymore. She gives us animals for food, but trophy hunting or collecting parts of animals for medicinal reasons will no longer be allowed. If anyone does, they will be answering to him," she said, nodding toward the Beastmaster. "I fear because of man's arrogant tendencies the underworld may get a lot of new residents in the next couple of months."

The people of Parliament were making wild gestures which Emily found quite amusing. After a moment of watching the crowd the old man moved up to the mic beside her. "Hear me and understand," he said, in a loud voice. "Cathleena loves all of her father's creations, and does not wish to harm anyone, but I will in her name if need be. So I say to you, fulfill her demands. If you need help with any of the tasks that have been given to you, all you need to do is ask, and we will come."

Chapter Eleven

Mr. Yates threw his jacket down on the couch next to his wife. Flames seemed to rise from his head, he was so angry. Mrs. Yates cowered behind a cushion and quickly turned off the TV. The so-called Goddess's demands were all over the news now. Granted, Parliament had kept the meeting between them and the Goddess's representatives/terrorist group quiet for some time, not wanting to alarm the public while they tried to figure out who they were and how to stop them. But once the dams started disappearing and people were living in the dark and unable to heat their homes or cook their meals, the government was forced to share the request of the supposedly returning goddess.

"What's wrong?" she asked meekly.

"Cathleena," he yelled. "Because of her, my company will be shutting down." He took several deep breaths to calm himself and then continued with his story. "I was told by government officials this morning that space exploration has been classified as non-essential, so there will be no more shuttle program. Therefore, they no longer have need for my rocket fuel. And besides all that, they decided to inform me that I will not be allotted any electricity to run my factories, because manufacturing a dirty energy is not considered by the government to be a necessity right now."

"Dirty?"

"Petroleum has been labeled as a dirty source of power, and people are being encouraged not to use it."

"Luckily we still have power."

"That's because your brother and his gang haven't hit the Lower Maygar dam yet."

"What of your plans?"

"My plans are on hold, obviously."

"What are we going to do if we lose power?"

"I can use my magic to keep everything going here, but it'll be too draining on my powers." Walking over to deck, he stepped out into the fresh spring air. Squaring his shoulders, he said. "I could try to stop them, but the last time I met your brother in combat, I underestimated him and died. Since then, I've made the grave mistake of tutoring him, which of course has made him even more powerful than before. No," he said shaking his head. "If I die again, I don't think Grandmother would be so willing to bring me back."

Yates thought for a moment, then turned to his wife. "Maybe it's time for a little family reunion."

"What am I to do against him? Cage him in vines? If you fear him, how am I to--?"

Yates silenced his wife with wave of his hand. As she struggled to bring air into her lungs, he closed in on her. "**I, do not, fear him!** And if you speak of it again, I will send you into the underworld to be with your mother." His shadow fell upon her as she started to lose consciousness. "He has allies," he whispered in her ear as he released his hold, allowing her to breathe. "I want him weakened. Befriend them, then come to me and we will make a plan to bring him down."

Aurelia rubbed her throat and sat up once more on the couch. "What of Cathleena? Even if you can defeat Sabvon…"

"I'll worry about Cathleena," he said patting her cheek. "I have an idea on how to deal with her."

"Folks are moving out of the big cities," Deb said, accepting a tray of fruit and bread. "The government is powerless, fights are breaking out, and people are being killed over food. It's really disheartening."

Emily placed her hand on Deb's arm. "We've spent over a year preparing them for this, we tried to warn them. We went to Parliament, we went to the papers, we went to the police, we went to the schools, and we went to all the different religious groups that are out there. We plastered the internet with Cathleena's demands before we slowly started cutting power. Don't feel too bad some people heeded our warning and have found sanction at some of the old sites, or have started their own little farming communities, and many smaller towns have switched to wind or solar power to keep their lights on."

"You don't understand, those are the people that are being killed right now. The ones that were smart and did what was asked of them, their farms are being overrun and taken away from them."

"No!" Emily sprang to her feet and called Tegula to her side. She knew of a little farming community just out of the Old forest of Dane that supplied a half dozen families with food and shelter.

The farm, which was a fifty by fifty meter lot, had rows and rows of corn, peas, cabbage, and other vegetables starting to grow in its center. Surrounding it were vehicles of all shapes and sizes that people used for housing, and three windmills for power.

Tegula pulled on Emily's leg as they appeared behind a maroon minivan. Looking out into the enclosure, she watched as a heavy set man pummeled the lead farmer with his fist. "Stop it!" she yelled, running around the minivan into the circle. "Leave him alone."

The heavy set man got off the unconscious farmer and turned on Emily. "Get her."

She didn't see them coming, but she felt the hands grabbing her. Flashes of the Beastmaster's battle with the government filled her mind, and she called forth the birds of the air to protect her. To her disappointment only a few crows showed up to squawk at the intruders from the roofs of the cars.

"We're hungry, we haven't eaten in days," the heavy set man said as he approached Emily. "These people won't share what they have."

"So you beat them senseless for food that's not even ready to eat yet?"

"They had some hidden. We just needed to persuade them into telling us where it was."

Emily felt Tegula touch her leg and pictured the other side of the compound. Popping in behind the heavy set man she grabbed a shovel off the ground and clobbered him in the back of the head, knocking him unconscious. The other two men became alarmed when they saw she was no longer in their grasp and rushed her. Again she disappeared and popped in behind them with the shovel, knocking one of them senseless before disappearing once again. As the last of the attackers turned around nervously looking for her, Emily reappeared quickly, hammering him in the head as well.

Clutching her weapon, she spun around as the crows again started to squawk loudly. Women and children were climbing out from under the vehicles that surrounded her. "Where are the men?" Emily shouted.

"Hunting. Johnson stayed behind to tend to the crops while the rest were gone."

Emily spun around, weapon in hand, when she felt the presence of another. Relaxing her grip, she sighed and looked at her master. "Why didn't they help me?" she said pointing at the crows.

"What did you ask them to do?"

"To do what those birds did for you the other day at the park."

The old man studied the birds, and then shook his head and looked at his apprentice, "They did not understand 'get them'."

Emily cursed under her breath," that's not what I said." She knelt down and checked the unconscious farmer. "I told them to help me."

A bird squawked from behind her, then another, and another. "Okay! Maybe I did say 'get them.' But come on," she said talking to the birds. "You knew I meant them, right?" she said pointing to the three bad guys. "Who else would I have meant?"

One bird hopped across the top of several cars and stopped behind the families of the farmers. After fluttering his wings, he squawked once more at her.

The group of women and children had a look of astonishment as they looked back and forth between Emily and the crow. Finally, a little girl said, "He's talking to you."

"Yes," Emily replied. "And not very nicely."

Turning to one of the adults, she added. "See to your injured and beware that there may be more of these type of men coming around."

The women nodded and gathered around the injured farmer.

Turning to the old man, she asked. "What are we going to do with them?"

"Take them to a place where they can't hurt anyone anymore."

With a wave of his hand, the old man gathered the bandits at his feet.

"How can he do that?" one of the woman asked.

"He's a son of a goddess," Emily said matter-of-factly, looking at the crows that were still sitting on the tops of the cars. *Watch over them, and tell me if there is danger,* she thought to the closest one.

The bird squawked as if understanding her command.

"Be careful," Emily said aloud to the women. "I'll check back with you later."

"Now that, they understood," he said, as she joined him. "Shall we?"

Emily thought of a place she'd been not so long ago and smiled. "I know exactly where to take them."

As they arrived the old man stood next to Emily with a sorrowful look on his face. Plains that were once lush grasslands and held an abundance of wildlife were now barren and desolate.

"I suggest that you and your friends start heading that way," Emily said, pointing over her left shoulder. "You have a long ways to go, and it's going to get dark soon enough. And just so you know, there are animals out here just as hungry as you. You preyed on the weak. Let's see how well you do when you're the prey."

The heavy set man rubbed his head as he looked over at Emily. "Where are we?"

"You're about 20 miles Northwest of Rainobi."

"What?! How in the--you can't just leave us out here. We'll die."

"I'm giving you more of a chance than you gave that farmer." Emily noticed the other two men getting to their feet. "I'd suggest you start moving. You've got about four hours before dark."

Construction was going well, and with the Beastmaster's help, the contractor had a pretty good idea on how to make Ciupap look more like its old self. Each series of terraces which were carved into the mountainside now held its own set of buildings and structures on them, and much like Cybele and Punasia, Ciupap was becoming self-sustaining once more.

Emily stood and watched a group of worker as the last of the thermal vents that would be supplying most of the heat for the settlement was being caped off.

"Excuse me," a meek voice said from below her. "I was hoping you could help me."

Emily turned to see young red headed women, about her height and weight standing on the twisting road below her. "Check in with the magistrate, she'll help you."

"I met you several years ago," the woman said as she started walking up the side of the hill. "It was when you first started preaching about conservation. You changed my life, you know. For the past four years, I've been studying Marine Ecology at the University of Santa Clara. I was an extern at the Pangaea Ocean Society, it was the best job I ever had. That was until they stopped sending ships out, and most of the buildings were closed down to conserve energy. Now I'm kinda at a loss of what to do. I'm done with school, and I can't find a job anywhere. I was hoping you'd be able to help me."

"Santa Clara, is Marshal still the Dean of Zoology there?"

The woman shook her head. "Never heard of a Marshal. Raphael was in charge when I was there."

Emily nodded. She'd had so many people trying to get close to her using the same old story of how they had known her from before. Some, like this woman just wanted a job, others actually tried to cause her harm. Not a good idea when you have a grumpy old demi-god watching over you.

Once the woman reached the spot where Emily stood, she reached out and shook her hand. "If what you say is true, you can take over some of the dates on my calendar for my conservation lectures."

"Wonderful. I'll be happy to help."

"I'm sorry I didn't catch your name?"

"It's Ariel Yates."

"It's a long ways from Santa Clara to the High Reaches. You must be tired and hungry."

"It took me three months to get here. Gas is harder to get and it's expensive so taking a bus, plane, or train was kind of out of the question. I tried hitchhiking, but there's not a lot of automobile traffic on the road anymore, and horse-drawn carts are not as charming as I thought they would be." She made a show of rubbing her backside.

"Yeah, but have you noticed how much cleaner the air is?"

Ariel nodded and looked out over the forested valley below them. "I've forgotten how beautiful the trees are here."

"You've been here before?"

Realizing what she had said, Ariel shook her head quickly. "I meant the mountains," she said sheepishly. "I've been on the coast for so long…there's not a lot of trees…well, you know what I mean."

Emily led Ariel down the twisted roads to a dining area on the lower tier. At first they talked about Ciupap and the hope for all the new colonies.

"We're trying to give people safe places to live. Ciupap is mixture of the old and the new," Emily explained. "Power here is derived from thermal energy, mostly.

"That should keep them toasty warm in the winter."

"Yeah, it's something that the ancients didn't know about this mountain, or they would have never abandoned it, I'm sure."

"So each structure has its own duct system?"

Emily nodded as they entered the main part of the settlement. "This is where the old meets the new. Each colony has its own smith, baker, cobbler, teacher, and a technical expert."

"Technical expert?"

"Some are computer experts, some are electricians. The buildings in the main square all have electricity."

"I don't see any wires."

"All underground."

"Why these buildings and not the others?"

"School, library, and government buildings are all down here. Once we get more wind and solar powered generators, the rest of colony will be hooked up."

"Sounds like you thought of everything."

"It has everything a self-sufficient village would need. Keeping the new is easy, it's teaching people the old ways that's hard, everyone who comes here is taught a trade. Like the old days, we have masters and they have apprentices. Knowledge will be shared and passed down from one generation to another. Every need is met. No one goes hungry here, and everyone is expected to do their share."

"So, does that mean you'll be my master? With the lectures and all?"

"I'll help you get started, but you're going to have to be the master and teach others." Emily saw the surprised look on her face and continued. "I'm sorry to throw this on you, but I've been looking for someone to take over the education portion of our rebuilding and mending process."

"What are you going to do?"

"Well, you could say I'm learning about animals. I myself have a master."

"Of what?"

"In the old days they called them Beastmasters."

"And who is your master?"

"The son of Adele."

"The goddess?"

Emily nodded.

"I would like to meet him, is he close by?"

"No, he's been spending a lot of time with the wizards from Cybele trying to clean up the Oceans. He pops in once in a while, but I haven't seen him for a couple of days."

"Oh well," she yawned. "Maybe next time."

"Let's get you a place to stay," Emily said waving over the magistrate. "Serena, this is Ariel, she's going to need a room for a couple of days. I'll take her back to Cybele with me when I leave on Tuesday."

Turning to Ariel, she said. "Enjoy dinner and get some rest. Tomorrow I'll start going over my lecture notes with you."

"How many?" the old man asked.

Emily sat within her circle, eyes closed, trying to sharpen her senses to the natural world around her. Silently, she made a kind of meditative call to the animals in her area.

"How many?" he repeated.

"Five. Four females, one male. A mouse, six anoles, and a mother sparrow with five eggs."

A stick came down hard, startling her. "I didn't ask for an inventory list of creatures in your circle. Just the sheep on the hillside. Let's continue. What else is on the hill with them?"

Emily cleared her mind and searched the hillside for other animals. Not far from the sheep hidden on a ledge above them, was a "Cougar!" she shouted.

"Reach out to her, see what she sees."

"What do you mean?"

"When you are one with the beast you can use their senses as your own, you can see what they see, smell what they smell, and hear what they hear. Their senses become your senses. Give it a try."

Emily sat for a moment, thinking about the cougar and how it would be nice to see what it was seeing. Suddenly the hillside became clear to her. She could see rocks and bushes, and could smell the sheep below her. She had a sense of motion as she and the cat moved quickly down the hillside toward their prey. They were jumping from one rock outcrop to another. She could see the cougar's paws out in front of her, swiping at a ewe, wounding it and knocking it off balance. She could sense the panic of the prey and smell the blood from the tear in its flank. She could see it in front of her and felt the surge as the cat leaped, locking its jaws around the ewe's neck and pinning it to the ground.

"Well," the old man said laying a hand on her shoulder. "Such is the circle of life."

Shaken, Emily turned to her master, wide eyed. "That was incredible, but freaky. Did you know that was going to happen?"

He started moving back toward the village, but stopped again after a short distance. "It's still hard for me to watch," he said softly. "Even though I know and understand that all of grandfather's creatures need to eat, it still bothers me to see one die." He turned toward her. "I think it's time for you to find your Hayat Hayvan."

"What's that?"

"A Life Animal. An animal that you can connect with. Sometimes, it's the abilities of the animal that will draw you to it. Like the eyesight of a hawk, or the agility of a gazelle, or the speed of a cheetah, or the power of a bear. You have a favorite animal, I assume, what is it?"

"I have several."

Returning to the circle, he settled down next to her. "Then tell me what they are and why you like them."

"Well," she said lowering her gaze. "I enjoy being around Manatees. I'm at peace when I'm with them. They're placid, nothing ever seems to bother them."

"Ah, yes, they are a peaceful creature, that is true. What other animals are you attracted to?"

"My next favorites would be the Northern Straits Orcas. Strong family groups, and powerful. They're mostly fish-eaters and I used to watch them all the time when they swam close to shore by my house. But they're gone now, so I guess I can't choose them."

"Those sound more like guides. You can have lots of animal guides throughout your lifetime. Sometimes animals come into your life for short periods of time, usually to help you through some kind of challenge or test that fate has thrown your way."

"So what was your Hait hayan…?"

"Hayat Hayvan. I've had many. When I was a child it was my dog Zorrie, and Leena, a horse. After they passed, it was Ada, Apep, and Zib-beno, Kurt and Ayi."

"Wow!"

"When you become one with an animal, and welcome it into your space, then you have found your Hayat Hayvan. Unlike guides who instruct you and help you navigate through life, Hayat Hayvans protect you and will help you reconnect with nature by reminding you that we are all interconnected. This is the way of the Beastmaster."

"But how will I know?"

"You'll know. Worry not, there are no right or wrong answers."

The pair started walking back along the path that led to the village. "Here are some questions to ask yourself. What animals interest me? Which frighten or intrigue me? Or if you dream about animals, what animal is always in that dream?"

Emily touched his arm and stopped walking. "There is one animal I can't get off my mind. It intrigues me. I think about it constantly, and I dream about it. But there's a problem. They don't exist on Valencia anymore."

Mr. Yates watched his wife venomously as she entered their living quarters, humming. "Where have you been?"

Happily, she placed her things down on the counter she leaned forward to kiss his cheek. As he pulled away, she sighed and said, "Giving lectures."

"Lectures?"

"On conservation. It's the job I've been assigned. It's the most fun I've had in years. You should see what they've been doing." Her excitement was apparent and she didn't let his scowling face deter her. "They're re-opening all those colonies we had started with Mother. Punasia and Ciupap are almost complete, and they have crews over at Xanila repairing what buildings they can, and tearing down and rebuilding the ones they can't repair. Their main focus is to get the rest of the world to learn to appreciate nature, and stop destroying it. People are encouraged to own horses again, to ride and use in their fields. Bicycles and skateboards are more popular than ever. Instead of factories, people are returning to specified traits like Stone Mason, Blacksmith, Tailor, Seamstress, and Carpenter." Suddenly she noticed some of her house plants showing signs of withering to lack of water due to her time away. Keeping her back to her husband, she moved around the house touching and bringing each plant back its jaunty self.

Feeling her mate's heated stare, she continued the conversation. "You know, like what Cybele was when we were last there. All colonies are self-sustainable, but they do encourage trade between the different settlements. I've been so busy, I've barely have had time to think. They have me hitting towns along the lower Maygar. They gave me a horse to ride, it's tied up outside. Anyways, I was in the area so I figured I'd stop in. I'm going to need more clothes." Mrs. Yates disappeared in the next room, and then continued the conversation when she returned as if there was no interruption. "For the last week, I've given four speeches on the protection and management of planet's ecosystems. I must say, Emily's papers are quite informative."

"Who?"

"My brother's apprentice. Her name is Emily. I've been told that he's training her to become a beastmaster."

Excitement filled his face. "Perfect, she's how we'll get to him."

"How? She's never alone, she has people around her all the time."

"You're going to get close to her," he said, closing the gap between. "You're going to become her best friend. And then you're going to bring her to me."

Chapter Twelve

Emily walked the last five feet across the white marbled floor to the center of the pavilion where Cathleena sat in the middle throne that was once occupied by her beloved sister Adele. On either side of her stood the Beastmaster and the goddess Ava.

"I feel like a kid being called into the principal's office." The look on all their faces told her that her joke went unappreciated. "So what's up?" she said with a quirky smile.

"I've been told that it's time for you to pick a Life Animal," Cathleena said, rising to her feet. "Since we are lacking in some species here, Ava has given permission for you to go to Terra in search of such an animal."

Emily tried not to show her excitement, but the smile beaming on her face was enough for all to know the joy that was in her heart. "When?"

"Now." Ava stepped forward and started a swirling fog around her.

Emily turned to her master. "Aren't you coming with me?"

"This is something you need to do for yourself."

"But..." Before she could finish her sentence, she was transported to the side of river on the outside of a rainforest somewhere on Terra. She had a feeling that she had been there before, but she couldn't remember on which trip. Looking around to get her bearings, she spotted movement on the far bank. Her heart skipped a beat as she watched a slick form disappearing into the thick vegetation on the river edge. "Of course," she shouted running along the river looking for a way across. "They knew. All of them knew. That's why they sent me here. They knew you would be here. But, how do I get over there?" Emily paced, staring across the water at the spot where there animal disappeared. Suddenly, a thought came to her. "You guys like water. Let's see if I can get you to come to me." Sitting down, she steadied the pounding in her heart and cleared her mind. Taking in a deep breath she reached out with her mind, searching for the big cat. Below her she sensed two river otters fishing for crayfish and playing at the water's edge. A couple of feet to the right of her was a burrow with a mother rabbit and her four kits. Behind her to the left she sensed…What was that behind her? It was a cat but she didn't know what kind. Excitement overtook her, she gave a little silent scream of joy in her head and started concentrating. She thought back to all the time she spent in the circle and everything that her master had taught her.

Eyes closed, take a deep breath, then another. In, and out. In, and out. Let go of the limitation of your physical body, reach out. Imagine the woods and the grasses around you, stretch out mind, and welcome the creatures of this world into your space. Gradually at first, then fairly rapidly, Emily's senses became overwhelmed with Terra's creatures. Unlike Valencia, they were everywhere and all very willing to become her friend. Disappointment set in as she tried pushing though the dozens upon dozens of animals milling around in her vicinity to contact the Jaguar she'd seen across the river.

Emily felt the wind picking up, brushing the side of her face, she felt the sun warming her back and the touch of something moving across her leg. After identifying the creature as a mouse, she reached out once again to encourage the large cat to cross the river. Minds, big ones, little ones, 20, 30, all touching hers, all sending signals of friendship and love.

Irritated, she opened her eyes. "Oh my!!!"

Cathleena moved silently up next to her sister at the edge of her pavilion on Terra. Looking across the glade, she spotted what held her attention. "You're peeking?"

Ava jolted upright and glanced over at her sister. "Don't you wonder what she'll pick?"

"I know what she wants to pick, but I know it's not what picks her. I think you'll be surprised at what our apprentice brings back with her."

"Tell me?"

Cathleena smiled. "Look for yourself."

Ava stared down onto her world. She could see Emily sitting near the river but couldn't see anything else. She shrugged.

"The Jaguar is there across the river, but he will not come to her. There's a larger cat that patrols those lands where Emily is sitting. But he will not be the one either."

"I see him," Ava squealed. "It's a big Tiger."

"A Boretra Tiger, lost from my world almost as long as the Jaguar she so desperately wants."

"But why won't he bond with her?"

"Because she has already bonded with another, and it's not his time to return to Valencia. But don't worry. Our young apprentice will be well pleased with her Life Animals."

"Animals?"

Cathleena laughed. "I will go retrieve her, you may inform our nephew of her return."

Ariel left the village and followed the path that led to a trickling creek outside of Cybele. There on its banks she spotted Emily and went over to her. "There you are," she shouted with a wave. "Got your message, but why did you want to meet way out here?"

A low growl met Ariel as she approached. "Oh, my. What have we got here?"

Emily sighed. "It's not exactly how I thought it would happen. There was so many."

Giggling she circled Emily and her new found friends, and took inventory of her collection. Perched on her left shoulder was a tiny owlet with grey speckled feathers and big yellow eyes, on her right shoulder sat a green Basilisk Lizard who liked to show off his double crest when you walked by. Beside her right thigh sat a young Margay, the object of the growls. Behind her, splashing in the creek noisily squawking, was Tegula with a mother pink-headed duck and her six fledglings.

"I practically had to run. If Cathleena hadn't gotten there when she did, I would be toting home a whole zoo."

Ariel knelt in front of the Margay, and made some soothing sounds at him. "Beautiful. It's like a little version of Ada."

"What did you say?"

Clearing her voice she said meekly, "It looks like the little leopard cub on the Beastmaster statue at the entrance of the city."

Emily's facial expression softened. "Yeah, I guess it does, but FYI, Ada was a Jaguar."

"Of course she was. I've heard the stories, I just forgot."

Responding to Ariel's soothing noises, the young Margay left Emily's side an approached the other woman. "Have you thought of names for them yet?"

"I thought they were supposed to tell me their names," Emily said jokingly.

"You know more about this than I do."

"That's just the problem, I don't. My master spends more time with his aunts and fixing the world than with me." Emily sighed and sat on the ground next to Ariel. "He used to spend more time with me, but…"

Both women ran their hands through the Margay's soft fur. "So you have a demi-god as a master, but you never talk about your family."

Taking the Basilisk off her shoulder, she set it down to let it join the others at the creek. "My master is my family. Somehow, in a weird sort of way, I'm related to him."

"You're from his line?"

"No, his sister's."

Shocked, Ariel's hand went to her mouth. Struggling to keep herself in check, she stood and moved a short distance away from Emily. In her head she thought, *he had a child. My beloved little boy had a child.* In a strained voice she asked. "How did you find that out?"

"His mother Adele told him." Emily looked over at the young lady, her back was to her but she could tell she was shaken. "Are you all right?"

Nodding, she calmed herself. "I was just thinking of my own family. Sorry, I didn't mean to get emotional."

"It's all right. It's understandable." Emily looked at the spot where Ariel had been sitting. The grass was thicker and greener from the patch she was sitting on. "That's odd."

"What's odd?"

Emily got to her feet and brushed herself off. "Never mind."

"Why did you ask me out here?" she asked, turning back to her. "To show me your new pets?"

"No, I wanted to let you know that I'm going to be heading to a place called the Sacred Valley. It's not very populated, and it'll give me a chance to get a handle on all this," She said pointing to the animals. "Plus I need to talk to some people up there."

"So, that means I'm going to be running everything now, as far as lectures go, I mean?"

"You already do. You're a great public speaker and through your words I can feel your conviction, dedication, and sincerity."

"You've heard me speak?"

"Many times." Emily started back down the path, calling her brood to follow her. "I love the ocean, and talking about it is one of my passions. But with you, it's the woods and forests. I heard you talk about deforestation. It brought me to tears. It was like I could hear each tree weep as it was being cut down. Powerful, you're a lot better speaker then I ever was."

"Thank you. That's very nice of you to say that."

"You should have been a botanist, or a master gardener. Hey maybe you could help the farmers around here. Do you know anything about crops?"

"Oh yes, lots. I love all plants. I would love to help. But what about the lecturing?"

"You'll have to recruit more people to take over, but for now I don't see why you couldn't do both in your travels. Stop at the farms along the way, see if you can help them out, and while you're there you can talk to them about conservation."

Ariel looked at her in astonishment. "I can't believe how nice you are to me."

"What? Why wouldn't I be? You're smart, sweet, and always eager to help. I only wish I had a dozen more like you." Emily gave the startled Ariel a hug, and then walked past her with her menagerie in tow.

Mrs. Yates stepped into her high price sophisticated home, seeing it in a totally different light. The elegant furnishings, the antique mirrors and vases, the priceless paintings, all had lost their luster in her eyes. Sitting on their expensive leather couch from Darlings was her husband, tipping back his glass of wine like he always did. "Why do we drink when alcohol doesn't affect us?"

Mr. Yates put his glass down and looked over at his wife.

"And do you realize you are sitting a dead animal there. I know at the store they said it was grained leather, but I can tell you for a fact that it's nothing more than genuine, maybe bonded."

"What has gotten into you?"

"And why," she said sweeping her arms around the room at the withered vegetation. "Can't you water my plants while I'm gone? It's not that hard to use the water can, or use your bloody magic, but do something, I'm tired of the death. I can't handle it anymore." Collapsing, she started to sob uncontrollably.

Picking up his glass again Mr. Yates leaned back and returned to watching the news. "They removed another dam yesterday, but today for spite I returned it. Let's see what your dear older brother thinks of that."

"Why fight them?" she said between the tears. "They're trying to help the planet."

Mr. Yates started rising out of his seat, glowing with an eerie red. "I don't care about this planet!" he shouted, blowing out the windows around him. Flicking his hand he sent a flame that covered the vegetation. "I don't give a dang about your plants and I definitely don't care that you're tired of all the death around us."

Mrs. Yates scrambled to get away, but her husband caught her with a magical force before she was able to leave the house. Slamming her against a wall, he heard the bones crack and break in her right arm. "I told you to bring her to me, and you disobeyed. Where is she?"

Aurelia shook her head feebly. "We can help, me with plants, you with your magic. They need more magic users to help clean up the planet."

He looked at her blankly, using the magical force around her body he started to squeeze like a giant python, forcing the air out of her lungs. Yorick was forcing the life out of his wife. "Where is she," he said. "Tell me and all will be forgiven."

"No."

"What is wrong with you, why would you die for this woman?"

Tears started streaming down Aurelia face, "She is from my blood. He lived, my baby lived, and he had children, and they had children and she is from one of them."

"So where is she?"

"I won't tell you."

"So be it."

Aurelia watched as her hands started to wrinkle and get age spots. She felt a weakness coming upon her, and looked toward her husband. "You'll never escape this world, and after Sabvon is don…"

He cut off her words as he cut off the air to her lungs. "Say hello to your mother."

Chapter Thirteen

Emily sat on the edge of the ancient walls that ran along the outskirts of the Sacred Village. 'Kedi', the name she had given her Margay, was at her feet playing with Tegula, and 'Peep', her little Owlet was sitting on the wall next to her, screeching at their antics. Suddenly Kedi growled and sprang to his feet, but before he or Tegula could move more than a foot, they were both turned to stone in front of her. Startled, Emily fell backwards off the wall, and gave Peep a mental command to go get help as she hit the ground.

"You are a hard person to track down," she heard a male voice say from her left. "Do you realize how many settlements I had to go to, and how many people I had to kill or torture to find out where you were?"

Emily scrambled to her feet, "Why, what did I do to you?"

A man dressed in suit and tie moved into view. "You, Cathleena, Sabvon. I never loved this planet, and I would prefer it the way it was. I did well for myself, helped technology along the way. So some trees got cut down, and few rivers got dammed. Big deal. Nobody was suffering from it, people were doing just fine."

"You call breathing polluted air fine, or drinking toxic water, or eating tainted food."

"Oh you see, none of that ever bothered me. I guess that's mostly because I'm not a wimpy human like you."

He's not human, she thought to herself. That means he's... "Yorick?"

"And you're Emily, great-great-great, whatever of Aurelia. Yeah, I heard."

"Hang around. I'm sure your cousin will be happy to see you again."

"I'm counting on it."

"What!"

"Yeah, you're not the one I'm really after."

"He kicked your butt once, he'll do it again."

"Now, it would have been best to not have reminded me of that."

Emily dodged a blast of energy and mentally called upon the animals in the valley to aid her.

Squirrels, rabbits, and lizards all ran at the mage, scratching and biting him all over.

Shaking his assailants off, Yorick took cover and shot spears of flames at the pests around him. Then, when given the chance, he threw another blast of energy at

Emily with explosive speed, this time hitting her in the chest and knocking the wind out of her.

A shriek filled the air as hundreds of birds of all sizes started dive-bombing the wizard, again forcing him to take cover.

In a flash that shook the earth, the old man appeared between Yorick and Emily. "Again, cousin. Must we really go through this again?" Before Yorick could answer, the Beastmaster sent a six foot chunk of tree flying at his opponent, which struck with a satisfying crunch. Yorick stumbled, and the old man sent a burst of blazing light, hitting again before he could recover from the first hit. Then calling upon the creatures of the woods, the Beastmaster sent wave after wave of biting insects over the dazed mage.

"Enough of this!" Yorick shouted, setting himself ablaze and killing his tiny attackers instantly, but causing no harm to himself. As the fire died, he turned back to the old man. "Is that the best you have, Beastmaster? Will you not use the wizard powers that our grandfather gave you, and I honed all those many years, to battle me properly? And I had such great hopes for you." Reinforcing his shield, Yorick braced himself against a tree and readied himself to send a blast of electricity at his foe, but before he could launch it, another multitude of birds hit him from the side.

The old man thanked Emily for the timely aerial assault. He was too old for this, he thought, becoming aware of how rapidly he was tiring. "It's not over yet cousin," he said disappearing from sight.

Yorick laughed out loud. "Your father tried this trick on me and it didn't w--." Before he could finish his sentence, chunks of earth bounced off his magical shield, again and again, hitting it over and over until it started weakening. Desperately, he threw out a ball of flame in the direction that the dirt had come from. It hit, and having his own magical shield damaged the old man was forced to reappear to repair, allowing Yorick time to send two consecutive energy blasts which knocked the Beastmaster down. Then he turned his attack on Emily. First her legs felt heavy, as though weighed down with lead. Then she realized with horror that her skin was darkening and changing. Frightened she twisted frantically, trying to move away from the encroaching porous material which was encasing her lower body.

Exhilarated by his triumphant moves, Yorick didn't notice the branches and vines zipping toward him from all sides. In fact, it wasn't until the vegetation had encased his chest and was closing him into a tight cocoon that he finally realized something was terribly wrong.

The old man looked behind him. Emily was up to her chin in stone. Turning to his cousin, he held out his hand. "Do you wish me to use my wizard skills, cousin? Perhaps I should tell you my name."

Arms pinned, and gagged by the plants, Yorick shook his head violently.

Sobbing, the old man made his way to his apprentice. The stone was making it hard for her to breathe and her skin had a tint of blue.

"Why can't you boys ever learn how to play nicely," a woman said in a lazy voice.

He'd heard that voice before in his youth. Spinning around, he turned to its owner. Before him stood three women, one dressed in a gown of scarlet, and two in white. A hand gently rested on his shoulder from behind as he searched the faces of the women in front of him.

Stepping forward, the woman in red spoke. "Well, isn't this an awkward family reunion."

"Will you restore her mother?" Cathleena asked moving beside Emily.

Nia drifted over to Emily, her skirts floating softly over ground. "So she is the child."

Removing her hood, Adele moved ahead as well. "Yes Mother, she is the one."

"Before I do it, what of your promise?"

"It's not his time yet. There still much for him to do."

"That was not what we agreed."

"You have Aurelia, why can't you be happy with that?"

Aurelia uncovered her head and looked over at her brother's saddened face. "I want to know what you're going to do with him," she said pointing over at Yorick.

Still trapped in his vine constructed cocoon Yorick turned away from his wife's angry gaze.

The old man interceded. "Let's not let her die because of your bickering. Please, Grandmother, remove the stone. Then we can decide mine and Yorick's fate."

"Oh very well." Nia lightly set her fingers on Emily's neck. A moment later the rock began to blister and crack, turning to white and falling off of her first in small pieces and then larger chunks. As the rock peeled away from her chest, Emily took in a huge, gasping breath. Caught in her master's arm she feebly pointed to the other side of the wall where Tegula and her Margay, Kedi, both rested encased in stone as well.

"Don't worry, we'll have them back to normal soon enough. Now rest."

After everyone was freed from everything which imprisoned them, Nia insisted on more comfortable surrounding for which to hold their business.

Emily sat out in the middle of the glade, brushing white dust off herself and her companions, and praising Peep for being so brave bringing help back so quickly. Glancing up she spotted the woman she had known as Ariel, except in a much older form, walking up to her. "I guess you're my great-great-great-great-great-great-great-great-great grandmother."

Aurelia nodded. "I guess so."

"So are you dead?"

"Yeah, looks that way."

"Bummer, I really could have used a Master Gardener."

"I'm glad I met you, Emily. If I hadn't, I would've continued on as Yorick's puppet."

"It was you who trapped him wasn't it?"

"I wasn't going to let him hurt my family."

"Did you know my mom and dad?"

"Dominic took our child to raise. I never got to watch him grow up. Even though I was a thousand years old, I was still naive and very impressionable. Yorick was already poisoning my mind, with his talk of grandeur. He wanted to be a god. Not here of course. He hated Valencia, he was an outsider. All he ever talked about was going off-world. Once the goddesses left he thought he could do with the shuttle program. But then you came around, and Cathleena came back, and you woke my brother up, and all that changed."

"They want to talk to you, Aurelia," the old man said, patting his sister's shoulder. Once she left, he turned to Emily. "Josiah and Stan were killed by Yorick. Along with a few folks from other settlements."

Emily stared at him in disbelief, and mumbled the words, "Oh no."

Raising his hand to calm her, he continued. "The goddess of the underworld has decided to return to the living any and all who were killed by Yorick's unprovoked attacks."

Drying her tear streaked face she said. "Please thank your grandmother for me."

"Mother. Grandmother has decided to leave the underworld for a while. Mother has agreed to take over. It's a way for her to still take care of her humans, even if it's after their deaths, she can still give them comfort and help them through the process."

"And you?"

"Well, she doesn't know it yet, but Aurelia and I are staying with you. There's still a lot of work around here to do."

"What about me?" a little voice from Emily's side said.

The old man brushed more powder off Tegula's shirt. "What, you don't think you're going to get out of all the work, do you? Next year we're going to start rebuilding the Ice Packs. I understand you have some understanding about refrigeration."

Emily touch her master's arm as he started to rise. "What's going to happen to Yorick?"

"He's always wanted to go off-world, so Grandmother is going to take him to his father. Jezekiel."

"That doesn't sound like much of a punishment."

"According to Mother, it'll be punishment enough."

The End

Made in the USA
San Bernardino, CA
02 May 2017